Four Pucking Christmases
CHICAGO RACKETEERS

EMMA FOXX

Copyright © 2023 by Blake Wilder Books

All rights reserved.

No part of this book may be reproduced in any form or by any electronic or mechanical means, including information storage and retrieval systems, without written permission from the author, except for the use of brief quotations in a book review.

Cover by Qamber Designs

About The Book

I always imagined bringing my hot, charming, amazing new boyfriend home for Christmas.

And I thought about how great it would be to meet his parents too.

But I never really thought about what that might look like if I was dating *three* men. Together. As in, what it would be like if we were all dating each other.

And now it's here. Our first Christmas. And our first chance to be together...with our families.

Four Christmases in two days.

Where's that spiked eggnog?

CHAPTER 1
Nathan

FORTUNATELY, two-thirds of the people who have regular slumber parties at my penthouse are not early risers. And the one who does get up early like I do is currently in the shower. I should be able to slip out before I see anyone this morning. I'll take care of my business, get it out of the way, and be back here with brunch groceries before Dani and Crew are even out of their pajamas.

I glance at the bed. Crew is spooning Danielle, his head buried in her neck, his hand splayed over her belly, their feet tangled under the duvet. Wrapped around our girl like that is his favorite place in the world, and it would take a not-so-minor earthquake to wake him up.

He's started saying that he can't sleep as well without her in his arms.

It's possible that he's saying it because he loves my sheets, and my rainfall shower, and my very expensive shower products.

But it's even more possible that it's the truth.

Because it's true for me.

Right now, I want to strip off my clothes and climb back into bed on her other side, where I sleep, and cuddle her soft, warm, sweet-smelling body up against me. Yes, I'll have to drape my arm over her next to Crew's, but I've gotten used to having another man's arm resting against mine in the night. Even another man's foot on mine. It's just how it goes when you're sleeping with a woman who's sleeping with two other men at the same time.

It's fine.

I'm saving on my heating bill, at least. Michael is like a furnace, and Crew is a cuddler, so when we're all in the same bed, it's plenty warm, even in Chicago in December.

Danielle made a soft grumbling noise, and her hand tightened on me when I slipped out of bed from her other side, but her eyes hadn't opened, and when I kissed her forehead and said, "Sleep, sweet girl," she'd sighed and smiled and burrowed deeper under the covers.

They're not going to catch me before I leave. Which is perfect. We have a big weekend ahead, and I need to take care of my own personal stuff before all of that starts.

It's December twenty-third, and after Crew's game tonight, we have three family Christmases ahead of us.

I take a deep breath. It's going to be fine. Great even. It's a holiday. It's bright and festive, and full of good cheer, and…

Who the fuck am I kidding?

I'm dreading this. All of it.

I'm not just going home to meet my girlfriend's family for the first time. I'm also meeting her two other boyfriends' families for the first time.

I shove a hand through my hair. How the hell is this my life?

For a guy who's always been pretty happy not forming ties and getting emotionally attached to the people I date, I've broken every rule and turned my back on everything I thought was common sense in relationships.

Because of Danielle Larkin.

I don't just have a serious girlfriend. I haven't just fallen head over heels in love for the first time. I haven't just gone from being completely alone and emotionally unavailable to thinking about moving her in with me, wedding rings, and the future in the course of two and a half months. I also have a relationship with two men who are also in love with her.

And it's working.

That might be the most startling thing about all of it. Having Crew and Michael as a part of all of this is fucking working. We're a family.

And for a guy who spent most of his life alone, I'm still trying to get used to it.

But damn, I like it.

Most days.

It's also coming with unique pressures and some complications.

Like Christmas.

For the past few years, it's been only my grandfather and me. Now I'm not just going to meet Dani's parents for the first time. We're also stopping by Crew's mom and dad's, where it will be his parents and his sister Luna, and God knows who else.

Then we're looping up through Indiana to see Dani's mom and dad and the extended family that always comes for Christmas Eve. I have no idea what to expect there.

After we spend the night there, we're stopping in Decatur to have Christmas Day brunch with Michael's family. Wouldn't you know that I would get involved in a poly relationship that includes a guy who is the oldest of six? I won't just be meeting his mom and dad for the first time, but all five of his sisters, their significant others, and several nieces and nephews.

I feel my gut clench.

I have been through a number of high-stakes, cutthroat business negotiations in my life. I've sat through very tense hockey games where my team could win or lose it all. I've sat at doctor's appointments and heard terrible news about my grandfather's health.

And I don't think I've ever been as tense as I am right now, thinking about the next two days and the three fucking Christmases that we're going to have to get through.

But I need to go see my grandfather first. I don't have a lot of family to bring into the chaos. Thankfully. At least I won't be contributing to this... Damn, even with my nerves about it all, I hesitate to call it a mess.

I'm about to meet the people who helped make Danielle, Crew, and Michael into the people they are. And those people are now the three most important people in my life.

But yeah, Nathan Armstrong, a forty-one-year-old billionaire, mature, grown-assed man, is nervous.

I grab my phone off the counter, tuck it into my pocket, and start for the door. My driver will be downstairs waiting for me. He'll take me to the nursing home, where Val is going to meet me. We'll talk with my grandfather for a little bit, and then I'll be able to swing by and pick up some food before coming back to the apartment.

"Where are you going?"

My hand is literally on the doorknob when I hear Michael's voice behind me.

I take a breath. Fuck.

I turn back. "Just out for a little bit."

"Great. I'll go with you. I wanted to grab some more stuff for brunch."

I was going to get the brunch stuff. Michael's the cook, so I don't mind being the one who grabs supplies. Of course, I could have someone do that for us. But there's something about being the one who picks out the food and drinks we enjoy together that I really enjoy. I guess it's my way of providing for the family.

That's also bizarre. I've always had other people shop for me and oftentimes cook for me as well.

Food is certainly something I enjoy in social settings and have used to impress people, and I definitely can tell the difference between an expensive steak and a cheap one. But since having people in my home more often, sharing meals with me, I've started to care more about being a part of it all.

I love that they all want to spend time at my apartment most often. It makes sense, of course. I have the most space. But both Michael and Crew make great money and have very nice apartments. There's just something about them all coming to my apartment that means a lot to me.

"I'm actually not going to the grocery store first," I tell Michael.

But even as I'm trying to think up an excuse to keep him in the apartment, I know it's not going to work. Crew is a little easier to distract, and I could just ask Danielle to leave it alone, and she would, but Michael is insightful. He can read us all. He'll know something's up.

"Where do you have to go?"

What's the point of lying? At some point, they're going to ask me if I'm going to see my grandfather. I'd be a real asshole if I didn't see him for Christmas.

But these three make me so happy. So much of our time together is fun and happy. I guess I'm hesitating to take them with me today because… it could be sad.

My grandfather may or may not be having a good day. He may not even know who I am. It's easy to go see him for Christmas on the twenty-third because he won't know that it's the twenty-third. We can tell him that it's Christmas Eve, or Christmas Day, or, hell, Easter, and he won't know the difference. And a couple of hours after my visit, he may not remember I was there.

I sigh. "I'm going to the nursing home. Valerie and I are going to see my grandfather this morning."

Michael's eyes widened. "Hell, Nathan. Give me a second. I'll go with you."

"You don't have to."

"Of course, I don't have to. I want to. You don't need to do that alone."

"I've done it alone a lot."

Michael's waist is just wrapped in a towel, but when he crosses his arms and looks pointedly at me, I know that I'm the one who is vulnerable here.

"Do you want to go alone?" Michael asks. "Really?"

Three months ago, I would've said, "Hell yes". I don't need other people. I'm used to being on my own. I can take care of myself.

That has changed. Quickly. And majorly.

"It's not a fun trip," I tell him. "It's not like the other Christmas trips we're going to make."

Michael nods. "I'm aware."

Michael has met my grandfather. Hughes was working for the Racketeers before the Alzheimer's got bad, back when my grandfather still came to the office sometimes. And Michael is a doctor. He understands better than anyone that there are good and bad days— good and bad times—even within the same day.

Danielle has also met my grandfather. She's come with me to visit several times and has experienced many of his moods. The good, the bad, and the ugly.

But Stanford adores her. Even when he's meeting her for the first time in his mind, he quickly warms up to her and finds her charming and lovely.

Of course, he does. She's adorable. She wraps him around her little finger over and over again.

I know exactly how that feels.

Crew is the only one who hasn't met him in person. Crew joined the team after my grandfather was…gone. My grandfather knows who Crew McNeill is, though. He watches Racketeers games when he's having a good day. Everyone in Chicago who's even a tiny sports fan knows who Crew McNeill is.

Actually, my grandfather would love to meet Crew.

Again, if he's having a good day.

"I just don't want you all to have to go. Danielle and Crew are still sleeping. And we're having brunch. And you have to be at the arena later—"

"And you're trying to protect us," Michael said. "But you

don't have to. We want to be there for you. You have to put up with all of our families."

I give him a half-smile. "Mine is just a little different."

"No family is perfect, Nathan. But the four of us have decided that we're in this together. The fun stuff and the shitty stuff. Please let me come."

I could probably handle having Michael along. He's a very calming presence. And his medical background means I won't have to explain anything or prepare him.

I give him a single nod. "Okay."

He turns on his heel and heads for the bedroom to get dressed.

But the next thing I hear is, "Come on, Cookie. Let's go, Crew. We gotta get up. Nathan needs us."

"What's going on?" Crew sounds groggy.

"We're going with Nathan to the nursing home," Michael says.

The closet door opens. They all brought their clothes for the next few days when they arrived yesterday. Crew just lives out of his duffle bag, but Michael hangs his clothes up when he brings things over.

"Oh, I didn't know." Danielle's soft voice slips out to me.

I feel myself smiling, even though I hate that Michael woke them up.

"He was trying to sneak out without us," Michael says.

"What? Why?" Crew asks.

I hear the rustling of the bed sheets, and I know that they're both getting up.

"Hey, it's Dr. Hughes," Michael says to someone.

I'm assuming he's on the phone.

"I need you to hold the car until we're all down there. Don't let Mr. Armstrong leave without us."

I roll my eyes. He just called my driver. Andrew works for me. I sign his paychecks. And his generous bonuses. He wouldn't directly defy me if I went downstairs and got in the car. But he knows Michael, Danielle, and Crew well by now, and I wouldn't put it past him to stall until they made it downstairs to go with me.

"Thanks, Andrew," Michael says.

"I can't believe he was going to go over there without us," Danielle says.

I do feel bad. A little bit. I've been something of a Grinch about this Christmas.

I've never decorated much in my apartment. It's always just been me. Even when my grandfather and I did spend time together during the holidays, we would just go to a restaurant for dinner. We didn't exchange gifts. What do you give a billionaire who loved hockey so much that he bought a team?

Before my grandmother died, we'd have dinner at their house, but it was prepared by a cook and was still somewhat formal. After she passed, my grandfather and I started spending the holidays in the Caribbean.

I haven't had a true, warm family Christmas since I was a kid.

There never seemed to be a reason to decorate the apartment. When Crew and Danielle mentioned putting up a tree, I said no. I didn't want needles all over the floor. Then I pointed out the fact that we would not actually be here on Christmas since we were going to see everyone's families.

So Crew had taken Danielle out to shop, and they had decorated her apartment. It now looks like the North Pole threw up in the tiny space above the bookshop and bakery where she and Luna live together. A lot of it has trickled down the stairs and spread out through the bookshop and bakery as well. There's tinsel and garland, brightly colored balls and snowflakes, huge stuffed reindeer, plastic Santas, felt gingerbread men, and Styrofoam candy canes everywhere.

We all spoil Danielle in our own ways, and even though making her apartment and bookshop into a mini replica of Santa's Village wasn't my style, I smile thinking of the two of them piling carts full of bright, gaudy Christmas decor, and bringing it all back to her place, and decorating. Crew's credit card has a very high limit on it as well, and when he spoils her, it's in a more colorful, loud, over-the-top way than what Michael or I do.

But he makes her smile, and that makes me smile.

It also keeps the stuffed reindeer and plastic Santas out of my apartment.

I glance over at the mantle above my fireplace.

Despite there not being an inch of her own living space not covered with fake snow and red and green felt and tinsel, Danielle has managed to get a little Christmas spirit in my apartment anyway.

Crew assured me that the tiny gold hooks they'd stuck to the edge of the mantel are removable. From those hooks now hang four stockings in varying Christmas patterns. There's one with each of our first initials on the fuzzy white trim. And she's added a simple garland to the top of the mantel. It is all understated and looks very nice. Nothing gaudy or over-the-top about it.

Looking at them makes my chest tight with emotion.

I haven't had a stocking since I was a kid.

Just then, Crew comes stumbling out of the bedroom. He's dressed in blue jeans, a sweatshirt, and sneakers. His hair is tousled, but the long shaggy curls always look a little mussed so maybe he did do something with it other than just roll out of bed.

He staggers for the refrigerator, yanks it open, and grabs a bottle of orange juice. He unscrews the top and tips it back, taking three long gulps. It's a full-sized bottle of orange juice that most people pour into glasses and share with their family, but we've given up on Crew not drinking straight out of the bottle and have simply labeled the side with CREW in black sharpie.

After he swallows, he looks at me. "Hey, man."

"Morning."

"So, what should I bring him?"

I frown. "Bring him? What do you mean?"

"We're going to see your grandfather for Christmas, right? I'm so sorry. I didn't even think of it. What should I bring him as a gift?"

I shake my head. "You don't need to bring him anything. He won't even know that it's Christmas."

"What? But we'll tell him, right?"

"We don't need to. We can just make it a visit. He won't remember anyway."

"Yeah, but for the ten or fifteen minutes or whatever, he will. It's Christmas, man." Crew spreads his arms wide. "Everybody deserves to have Christmas, even if it's only for a few minutes."

I stare at the younger man. The much younger man. Literally, I could be this guy's father. He drives me crazy. He seriously does. A lot of the time, I want to smack him. But I have to admit, not only is he my star player, and the one who is very likely taking us to the Stanley Cup this year, he makes the woman I'm in love with deliriously happy.

And dammit, he makes me happy.

I might roll my eyes and shake my head, a lot, but I also smile and laugh a lot more since Crew McNeill became more to me than just one of my players.

Not that I am ever going to tell him that.

"He's going to be pretty excited to meet you," I finally admit. "He's a fan."

Crew grins a grin that clearly says, of-course-he-is. He tips back the orange juice and takes another swallow. "I'll sign a jersey," he says after swallowing.

"My grandfather used to own the team. He has more signed jerseys than he knows what to do with."

"But he doesn't have a signed jersey from me." He thinks for a second. Then he says, "How about skates? I just got new ones. Still have my last pair. Those are a lot harder to come by than jerseys."

I open my mouth to argue with him. I intend to tell him that, again, my grandfather won't remember that he even has the skates. Crew should keep those and give them to a charity auction or some kid with cancer or something. But then Crew's words about even five minutes of Christmas come back to me. Even five minutes of meeting his new favorite player and getting a pair of signed skates would give my grandfather immense joy. My grandfather could easily revert back to his forty-year-old self. Or his twenty-year-old self. Or possibly his ten-year-old self. He's been a hockey fan his whole life.

And then I could show him those skates again next week. And the week after. He could have those five minutes of joy again and again.

I feel my chest tighten as I also realize that I can always give those skates to charity someday...when my grandfather is gone.

I suck in a breath. Hell, I'll write a check to a kids' cancer charity today and give my grandfather some Christmas joy at the same time.

"Okay. He'd love that," I finally say.

"Cool. We'll swing by my place," Crew says easily.

Danielle walks into the room just then. She comes straight to me. "Good morning," she says sweetly as she wraps her arms around me.

I dip my head, putting my nose into her hair and breathing deeply. "Good morning. I didn't mean to wake you up."

"I know. And we might talk about that later, because you should have woken us all up. But for now, let's go see Stanford." She pulls back and looks up at me. "Okay?"

I know she's not asking if I'm okay. She's asking if it's okay if they all come along. I know that if I say no, Danielle will go to bat and try to talk the other guys out of it. But the thing is, I've come to trust Michael. I've always been the guy in charge. I make big decisions that affect people's lives every day. I'm known for my cool thinking, my ability to see the big picture, no matter the tiny distracting details, and I will make the decision for the greater good, the entire team, every time.

But when it comes to my personal life, I'm not so good at that. I have come to trust Hughes to be our voice of reason. He's someone I can actually lean on and trust to help with those decisions when my emotions are involved. I've never had a friend like Michael Hughes before.

If he thinks they all should come with me today, I believe him. And maybe it's not just for me. Maybe it's for them too.

I nod and lean in to give her a soft kiss. "Yes, it's okay."

We're all going to be meeting each other's families. We're all going to be getting some insight into what makes the others tick. For better or worse.

CHAPTER 2

NATHAN'S GRANDFATHER, Stanford, is having a good day, much to my relief. These visits are bittersweet for Nathan on a regular day of the week, but seeing the upscale nursing facility cheerfully decorated for Christmas is just another reminder of all he's lost.

But maybe, this year, it's a reminder of what he's gained as well.

Us.

The thought of all of us, and how in love with these men I am, makes this first Christmas together even more special.

Whereas normally Nathan strides down the hallway silently, alone, to his grandfather's room, we're a boisterous foursome today, gifts in hand, Crew in a Santa hat.

The Santa hat Nathan is eyeing with annoyance. "I told you not to wear that."

"Jealous? I'll let you borrow it." Crew plucks it off his head and tries to put it on Nathan, who bats him away.

Before they can have one of their disagreements that aren't really disagreements so much as their way of showing affection, they're interrupted.

"Aren't you Crew McNeill?" a man pushing a cart along the hallway asks, stopping and giving him a grin.

"Yes, I am," Crew says, holding his hand out. "Pleasure to meet you, man."

"Holy shit, this is crazy," the guy says, shaking his hand. "I'm a huge Racketeers fan. Are you ready for Charlotte tonight? Their goalie is on fire."

Crew gives him a cocky shrug. "But so am I."

The guy laughs. "Damn. I'm Dave. It's so cool to meet you. Can I get a selfie with you?"

"Absolutely, get over here. Santa hat or no Santa hat?"

"One hundred percent the hat."

"See?" Crew tells Nathan, who snorts.

"I'll take the pic," I offer, holding my hand out for Dave's phone. It still startles me, but I'm getting used to random people approaching Crew wanting an autograph or a selfie. They're always excited, and they walk away even more so because Crew loves this aspect of his chosen career. He's amazing at making fans feel special and appreciated.

"This is my girlfriend, Dani," Crew tells Dave. "And Nathan Armstrong, the owner of the Racketeers, and Dr. Michael Hughes, the team physician."

Dave's eyes widen. "Holy shit," he repeats. He shoves his phone at me. "It's nice to meet you. I've seen you on social media at games and... stuff."

By stuff, I'm assuming he's meant the various supportive and a few disapproving comments online about my relationship with the guys. Occasionally, there have been some hateful remarks, but most people seem to eat up our hockey romance.

"Don't believe everything you read online," Nathan says.

Dave laughs nervously. "No shit."

"Get in there," I tell him, giving him a smile. "And thank you for all the hard work you do here at the nursing facility. We're so appreciative of the care all the residents receive."

"Oh, I'm just a janitor," he said with a shrug.

"Everyone's job here is important. This is home for these residents, and you have a hand in making it clean and comfortable for them."

"Thanks," Dave says, giving me a nod and a smile.

"Okay, say Merry Christmas," I tell him, and I gesture for him and Crew to get closer. Crew throws his arm around Dave's shoulders and gives a smile. "One, two, three—

"Merry Christmas," they both say dutifully.

"Can I get one with all of you guys?" Dave asks. "Just really quick, I promise."

"Sure," Michael says.

"Even me?" I ask, a little surprised.

"Hell, yes," Dave nods. "You're the most famous girlfriend in hockey. My sister talks about how lucky you are all the time."

That makes my cheeks heat. I guess I knew that, but hearing it out loud is odd. I don't dislike it. Quite the opposite. "Well. Okay. Of course."

Dave jogs off to grab a nurse, who dutifully comes over to take our picture with him.

Finally, we're on our way again, and we enter Stanford's room. Val, Stanford's former secretary, and Nathan's surrogate family, is already there. Her eyebrows shoot up when she sees all of us, but she's clearly pleased as she smiles and waves as our entourage files in.

Michael is carrying a box from Books and Buns containing the chocolate chip cookies I know from past visits Stanford loves. Crew has managed to put his skates in a gift bag we picked up at a drug store on the way, and I have a poinsettia.

Nathan tolerates a hug from Val, but he looks self-conscious. I know it's hard for him to be vulnerable.

We're all about to spend the next three days being vulnerable as hell because four Christmases is a lot to handle, even if it is an exciting step forward in our relationship. I suspect the way Nathan looks now is how I'm going to feel when we walk into my parents' house tomorrow. Nervous. Awkward.

Uncertain what to say. Worried about what my family will say.

My parents know about my boyfriends because I finally told them two weeks ago, but they don't really approve, and they definitely don't understand. They find it hard to wrap their heads around, and I know they think–or at least hope–that this is some wild phase I'm going through and it will eventually end. Yes, I'm worried Christmas Eve will be a disaster.

But that's tomorrow. Right now, I need to focus on reassuring Nathan that we're all happy to be here with him.

I don't really need to, though. Crew and Michael have it all under control.

As I give Val a hug, Crew is already shaking Stanford's hand and buttering him up. "Mr. Armstrong, sir, it's an honor. Thank you for all you've done for the Racketeers. I love this team with my whole damn heart."

Stanford is smiling back at him. "Excellent. It's a pleasure to meet you, kid. I've been watching you all season, and you've got a hell of a future here with the franchise. We haven't won a championship since 1967, so I want you to bring one home for me before I die."

For once, Crew looks sheepish and a little in awe.

"I think Stanford Armstrong is the only person on earth who can render McNeill speechless," Michael murmurs to me.

I laugh softly. "I think you're right."

"Yes, sir, absolutely, sir," Crew finally says, nodding rapidly. "I'll give it everything I've got. Sir."

"Why does he get to be called 'sir' and you call me Nate?" Nathan asks. "Why don't I get that kind of respect?"

"Because you're a damned grump," Stanford tells him before Crew can reply.

Nathan snorts.

"I still can't figure out how you scored this sweet and beautiful woman." Stanford holds his hand out for me with a smile.

I smile back, my throat tightening as I take his hand. Stanford really is a lovely man. I wish so much that I could have known him before he got so frail and before his mind would wander so easily. I would have loved to hear all of his stories.

"I can't either, Stan," Nathan says, watching us with a bemused expression.

I've never known anyone who calls their grandfather by his first name, but Nathan said he got in the habit of it in his twenties because of keeping things professional within the Racketeers organization.

I squeeze Stanford's hand. "I'm the lucky one. Your grandson is an amazing man."

"Well, I really like him, and I'm glad you feel that way." Stanford tugs me down to sit on the ottoman next to his chair, still holding my hand.

I feel Nathan move in behind me, and his hand on my shoulder. I look up at him, and we share a smile, and I see the love in his eyes.

Crew takes a seat on the sofa next to Val. She beams at him.

I blink. Val never beams at anyone.

"You're doin' good, kid," she tells him.

Crew pushes his hair back from his face and gives her a smile. God, he's so cute when he's a little bashful.

Michael steps forward and extends the box of cookies. "Merry Christmas, Stanford."

Stanford looks up at him, his eyes widening. "It's Christmas?"

Michael nods. "It sure is. My favorite holiday."

Stanford takes the box, and Michael pulls another chair up closer to our group. I reach out and take his hand. He gives me a wink as we link our fingers.

Stanford opens the box. "Chocolate chip!" he exclaims. "My favorite."

"That's what Nathan said," Michael tells him with a nod.

Stanford looks up at Nathan. "You knew that?"

"Of course," Nathan says. "You…" He clears his throat, and I reach up to cover his hand with mine. "You used to bring chocolate chip cookies to the owner's box to share with me during games."

My heart squeezes. He didn't tell us that when he said he wanted to stop by the bakery for cookies.

Stanford nods slowly, his eyes focused on the wall past Michael, as if lost in thought. "You didn't like any of the food we offered at the concession stands or that we catered into the owner's box," he said.

Nathan clears his throat again. "That's right."

I want to hug them both. I love that they're sharing this memory, and that Nathan is seeing Stanford remember something sweet about his childhood.

Crew chuckles. "You didn't like pizza and hot dogs? Even as a kid?"

I look up. Nathan is actually smiling. "I didn't."

Michael addresses Stanford. "What did Nathan eat as a kid? When he was eight or nine? Please tell me he at least liked peanut butter and jelly."

Stanford nods his head. "Yes. And no." He leans closer to Michael. "But he only likes freshly made peanut butter, not store-bought. That's the fault of the cook we had when he was about six. She made it from scratch and insisted it was the best way, and he believed her. And he only likes jams because that sounds fancier. He also only likes it on biscuits or croissants."

"Oh for…" Nathan mutters.

I'm pressing my lips together, trying not to laugh.

Crew isn't even trying to pretend not to laugh. He laughs out loud. "Why am I not surprised you were pretentious even as a kid?"

"That was a long time ago," Nathan protests. "I was influenced by a lot of books and movies. And I've…loosened up."

But even he hesitates to say that about himself, and again, Crew laughs.

"Just last year, you would only eat orange marmalade," Stanford says, chuckling with Crew.

I look from him to Nathan. Nathan is looking at his grandfather with a mix of affection and sadness. I'm guessing that wasn't just last year.

Stanford is starting to slip a bit. All of the excitement of having us all here and finding out it's Christmas is maybe confusing him a bit.

"I had an orange marmalade period too," Michael says.

I look over at him. "Really?"

"Paddington," he says. He looks up at Nathan. "Right?"

"Right," Nathan replies, his voice a little gruff.

Oh, I love my nerdy bookworm boyfriend so much. Not just that he's read so much and fondly remembers details from childhood books, but that he can use those details to support Nathan.

"I also begged my parents to let me try Turkish delight and egg creams because of books," Michael tells Stanford. He shakes his head. "Was disappointed every time."

Stanford chuckles, but Nathan says, "I loved *The Lion, the Witch, and the Wardrobe*. And I finally found great Turkish delight in New York City after trying it several times because of Narnia." He clears his throat again, and I reach up to squeeze his hand. "I'll take you to that shop sometime," he tells Michael, squeezing me back.

Michael grins at him. "Can't wait. And if you've ever found a good cream cheese and liverwurst sandwich, I'd love to know."

Nathan shudders. "I quit trying after one of those." Now he finally chuckles himself. "No matter how much I loved *A Wrinkle in Time*, I just couldn't agree with Meg on that one."

"Cynthia can make anything taste good," Stanford says. "Even liverwurst."

"Who's Cynthia?" Crew asks.

"Our cook," Stanford says.

"She was," Nathan says quietly. "Thirty years ago." He directs it to Crew, but Stanford hears him.

"What do you mean? She made my breakfast this morning,"

Stanford says, frowning. "She always makes my eggs just how I like them."

I know from experience that it's better to just go along with him when he gets his timing mixed up. Arguing simply doesn't matter. And one of the sweetest things I've seen is how gentle Nathan is with him, even when I know it breaks his heart.

"She makes perfectly poached eggs," Nathan agrees, easily switching gears. "And her hollandaise sauce is excellent."

"Oh, you are so an eggs benedict guy," Crew says, also adjusting on the fly. He leans in toward Stanford. "But so am I." He winks.

Stanford grins. "I like mine with smoked salmon instead of ham."

"Never had it that way," Crew says. "But I have had it with pulled pork instead." He puts his fingers to his lips and kisses the tips with a smack. "Delicious."

"I'll have to make you eggs benedict my way," Michael says. "I use crab cakes."

Crew grasps Michael's arm with one hand and puts the other over his own heart. "Yes. Oh my God, yes."

"I want to try that too," Stanford says. "That sounds amazing."

"Michael's an amazing cook," I tell him. "You need to try his stuffed French toast too."

"I can't wait," Stanford says. "I love brunch."

"Me too," I tell him. And I do. I've always loved brunch, but since Michael became my personal chef, I *really* love brunch. And I'm even willing to give up the regular naked brunches we have at Nathan's if Stanford is able to come.

"Oh, Stanford, hey, I brought you something," Crew says, reaching for the gift bag. He slides it across the floor to set it at Stanford's feet.

Stanford's eyes light up. "A Christmas present?"

"Yep," Crew tells him. "I hope you like it."

Stanford leans over and digs through the black and silver

tissue paper Crew and Michael stuffed in on top of the skates. He withdraws a skate, holds it up, and reads Crew's signature.

His eyes widen, and he looks up at Nathan. "Look at this!"

Nathan smiles and nods. "Pretty great, right?"

Stanford looks at Crew again. "You got me skates signed by Andrew Mars? That's amazing!"

He really does look like a little kid in that moment.

Crew opens his mouth, but Nathan says quickly, "Of course. He's your favorite hockey player, right?"

"Definitely!"

Crew clamps his mouth shut. Nathan is grinning, and I know it's in part because his grandfather is so happy. But it's also because Stanford is excited over a different hockey player now.

I can't wait to hear the banter between these two about this.

We visit for another thirty minutes, enjoying the cookies and listening to Stanford talk about Andrew Mars who was, evidently, an amazing hockey forward in the nineties that Stanford tried to recruit, unsuccessfully, to the Racketeers for years.

We finally decide it's time to go when Stanford starts to nod off. Crew and Michael both shake Stanford's hand. I hug him and give him a kiss on the cheek, and watch Nathan hug him as well. Val leans over and hugs him, and whispers something in his ear.

Then Stanford calls out, "Kick ass tonight, McNeill!"

Crew and Michael are nearly to the door. Crew stops and turns back with a grin. "Will do, Mr. Armstrong."

"You know my birthday is next month," Stanford says.

Crew pauses and glances at Nathan. Nathan gives him a slight shake that says that's not true. Crew still grins at Stanford. "Let me guess, you want more cookies when I come back to visit for your birthday?"

Stanford nods. "Yes! But also…maybe you could sign something for me. You're one of my favorite players too."

Crew looks surprised. Then, making my heart melt, he blushes. He actually blushes. "I would be honored to sign something for you, Mr. Armstrong."

"Call me Stanford."

Crew tips his head. "Okay. See you soon, Stanford."

Crew turns to head out, with Michael falling in step beside him. Nathan and I are right behind them. I feel like I need to have my arm around Nathan right now. These visits always take a lot out of him, and I love the realization that I actually make him feel better.

When we get to the car, Nathan reaches up and claps Crew on the shoulder.

Crew looks over with a brow up.

"Thanks," Nathan says simply.

I wait for Crew to tease him or say something flippant. Instead, Crew pulls Nathan in for a bro hug. He pats him on the back and says, "It was my pleasure."

Then Crew climbs into the SUV.

Nathan takes a deep breath. Michael gives him a smile and also gives him one of those one-armed-half-hugs that men do. "Thanks for letting us come along." Then he rounds the vehicle and gets in.

Nathan is just standing there, and I tug on his coat sleeve. "Hey."

He looks down.

"You okay?" I ask.

He takes a deep breath and then nods. "I'm…really okay."

I smile and lift up to press a quick kiss to his lips. "I love you."

"I love you, too."

I start to turn toward the SUV to also get in, but Nathan grabs my hand and tugs me back to face him. He lifts his hand to my face. "I really love you, Dani. Thank you."

I frown. "For what?"

"For…being my family. For showing me that I wanted that again. For making me see that I could have it again when I didn't believe it."

I feel my eyes stinging slightly. "Thank you for letting me. And for being open to this family."

He glances at the SUV. "They were really great."

"They love you too."

He takes a deep breath and nods. "Yeah. I'm…"

"What?" I ask.

"Actually looking forward to the next couple of days. Meeting all of your families and everything."

I laugh. "You say that now." I lift up and kiss him on the cheek, then turn for the SUV. "But no matter what happens, you can't get out of this now." I glance over my shoulder at him and give him a wink. "And you have to bring Crew and Michael back to see Stanford for his birthday next month. You know Crew won't forget."

CHAPTER 3
Crew

I NEED a little post-game love from my girl. I always get energized (or pissed if we lose) after a game, and tonight I'm keyed up. We're killing it this season, and I can practically smell the playoffs. The only thing I want more than a shot at that cup is my girl.

Our girl.

"Honey, I'm home! Give your favorite hockey player a victory kiss," I announce as Doc and I arrive back at Nathan's place. She left right after the game with Nathan, worried about having enough time to pack for our holiday house-hopping festivities. "Who's ready for a road trip?"

My answer is a soft, low moan, and I'm greeted with the perfect shot of Dani laid out on the kitchen island. She's still wearing her sweater, but it's pushed up, and her jeans are on the floor by Nathan's feet. Her ankles are propped on Nathan's shoulders, and her cheeks are flushed as his tongue works her clit. Lust kicks me in the gut.

Now that's the way to kick off the holiday break.

I turn to Michael and raise an eyebrow. "Looks like the party got started without us."

"Looks that way." He clears his throat as he yanks off his overcoat. "There's a joke about packing somewhere here, but I don't care."

"Same." I take my own coat and shoes off, never taking my eyes away from Dani and Nathan.

"Hi, guys," she says breathlessly, forcing her eyes open to greet us. "Great game, Crew. I'm so proud—oh, God!—

Her sentence is cut off as she bucks her hips, blindly grasping for Nathan. "Yes, yes, Nathan, please, yes," she cries out as she explodes in an orgasm.

Dani grips Nathan's hair and grinds him deeper down into her pussy, and I rub my cock through my pants, so fucking turned on by how beautiful she is in her passion. Watching her grow into who she is, uninhibited and fully enjoying sex, has been amazing to watch.

Even with Nathan, that bossy bastard.

Not that I actually care, but I can read that motherfucker like a book. When we first all got together with Dani, he would do things out of jealousy. Now I like to think it's more a form of teasing me, and maybe a way to assert his position as boss.

"He did that on purpose, didn't he?" I ask Michael, sparing a glance in his direction.

Hughes gives a tight nod. "Oh, hell, yeah, he did."

We're both striding over to them, intent on getting in on the action, when Nathan pulls back with a smug smirk on his face. "Do what? Get our sexy little slut ready for you both?"

"Make her come in the middle of her compliment to me."

"What are you talking about?" he asks, straightening up and easing Dani's legs onto the island. "That never occurred to me."

He does a decent job of sounding innocent. But he's full of shit. He knew exactly what he was doing.

"Here, sweetheart," he adds, as if he's the most congenial motherfucker on the planet, "time for McNeill and Hughes to taste you too."

Dani nods eagerly and reaches her hand toward the two of us. "Come here."

Peeling my shirt off, I gesture for Michael to take her outstretched hand as Nathan strips her sweater off and tosses it to the floor.

"Go for it, Doc," I tell him. "Merry Christmas."

Michael is so easygoing that he tends to hang back and let me and Nathan greedily do whatever we want with our sweet Dani. He may be our calming influence and mediator, but that's all the more reason we should give him more consideration so we don't take him for granted. It's something I've been working on because I'm definitely aware that I'm not the most mature person in this relationship. I want to do this right so we can keep it going. Forever, if I have my way.

Damn, I fucking love this woman, I think as I watch Michael give Dani a slow, teasing kiss on the lips before he drops down and shifts his head between her thighs. Then I can see his tongue easing in and out of her pink pussy and how her thighs clench in response. My cock throbs, so I reach for my belt buckle, yanking it open.

"Jesus, Dani, I can see how wet you are from here. You're so fucking hot and wet that pretty little pussy is just dripping down onto Doc's tongue."

"I'm so wet," she agrees, her voice so excited and eager as I take my zipper down. "Michael, yes, that's just perfect—oh, my God."

The way she freely and enthusiastically invites Michael into her, the way she spreads her legs further and runs her fingernails across his scalp, and her heels dig into his shoulders, is sexy as hell.

"How does she taste, Doc?" I wrap my fist around my throbbing cock at the base of my shaft, studying Dani intently.

"Like the sweetest cookie I've ever eaten," he murmurs, lifting his chin up and down to tickle her soft thighs with his beard the way Dani likes.

It gives her goosebumps on cue.

Nathan is leaning on the island, fully dressed, and he digs his fingers into Dani's wavy red hair, forcing her to turn toward him. "Kiss me," he demands. "Taste yourself on me because Hughes is right—your pussy is as sweet as candy, baby."

Moving in on the other side of Dani's thighs, I fully enjoy the view. Nathan's tongue teases between her lips as Michael's flicks over her clit. I casually reach out and take one of her tight nipples between my thumb and forefinger and roll it. Dani gasps in approval, momentarily breaking the kiss with Nathan before he drags her back in.

She's stopped wearing panties at our request. Or command. The thought makes me grin a little. Dani likes being told what to do, and I find that sexy as fuck. She skips the bra too when she's layered up like she is today. She's wearing a tank top under her festive red sweater, and it's still shoved up over the peaks of her breasts.

"Thanks for getting these out for me to play with, Nate," I murmur as I pinch harder, then soothe the sting by enclosing my mouth over it and suckling it gently.

Adding my mouth to the mix changes the timbre of her breathing. She's quivering and panting. Closing my eyes, I revel in that sound. I flick my tongue over the curve of her breast as I move my hand up and down on my hard cock. She tastes so good, her skin so smooth and soft that my need intensifies. I want a kiss, that intimate connection that she manages to share with all of us with ease.

I tap Nathan on the shoulder. "Switch with me, Boss."

He does without hesitation. He really is in the holiday spirit today. I may have to ask him to drive his car later before his awesome mood evaporates. Which it will once he both sees my surprise tomorrow and he's forced to endure three Christmases with people he's never met.

Dani is reaching for me. "Crew. Kiss me."

I want to more than anything, but I've learned to read her body and her voice. She's on the verge of coming again. That little tremble in her thighs, the raspberry bloom across her cleavage, her head lolling back, and the hitch in her voice are all giveaways. A little teasing right now will go a long way in making her orgasm as hot and intense as possible.

She jolts a little when Nathan takes her other nipple into his mouth with a, "You like that, baby?"

"Oh, yes."

Doc is stroking his tongue in and out of her like a champ, and he's added his thumb, which explains her hips rocking and her back arching.

"I'll kiss you in a second," I tell her. "Come for Doc, baby. I can see how much you need to. Don't hold back."

Nate understands what needs to happen. This one belongs to Doc. Nathan eases off of her right as Michael shifts his tongue to her clit and hooks a second finger inside of her. Dani almost levitates off the island as she bursts apart like the firecracker she is, a cry of "Michael!" flying off of her lips. Nathan holds her firmly in place so she doesn't accidentally disengage Doc's tongue as she shakes and screams through a powerful orgasm.

"Oh, fuck yeah," I growl, stroking my dick harder and harder. I can't even comprehend how hot this woman is. "Now I'll kiss you." I take her mouth, hard, wanting her to pant and cry the remnants of her orgasm into my kiss.

As she opens for me, I grip her hand and pull it down onto my cock, moving her up and down my hard length. "That's it. Touch me while you come down."

"Damn, Cookie," Michael says. "That was sugar and spice, baby."

I sense him rising to his feet. My eyes are closed as I pour myself into the embrace, pumping Dani's petite hand harder and harder over me. I need more. I need all of her. I'm barely aware of my other hand seeking out her breast, cupping soft flesh, and squeezing hard. I need to fuck her.

I'm pulling my dick out when Nathan interrupts me.

"McNeill, bedroom, now," Nathan orders.

He's right. It's easier for Dani to take all three of us on the bed. With extreme willpower I rip myself away from her.

Dani is primed for more. She's all pink cheeks and goosebumps, her eyes glazed over with desire. Her legs are slack, her chest heaving up and down. Her pussy is all pretty and pink, moisture trailing down her inner thigh that I want to lap up.

Michael raises his fingers and sucks the essence of Dani off of him. I almost moan, jealous, but in a good fucking way. I'm not a patient guy, but I know I'll get my turn to taste her sweet little pussy, if not tonight, then tomorrow, and it will be worth the wait.

I do bend over and indulge in flicking my tongue over her tangy sweetness easing down her thigh. She shivers and reaches for me, trying to direct my head between her legs.

"Nope." I stand back up. "Get over here, gorgeous," I tell her as I scoop her up. "Let's go where we can all worship you head to toe."

She wraps her arms around my neck and her legs around my waist. Her nipples brush against my bare skin as she turns, questing for another kiss. Her lips are swollen and shiny, and I know exactly what I want next— my dick sliding in between them. I want to watch her eyes go wide and tear up as she chokes on my cock. Dani is always ready and willing to take me deep.

I give her the kiss she's seeking, but then I turn back to Nathan and lift her up a little under her knees to display her backside. "Seems to me there's a hot little ass hanging out that might need to be spanked."

"You read my mind," Nathan says, rubbing his jaw as he stares intently at Dani's bare flesh.

"What did I do?" Dani asks, sounding full of fake concern.

Nathan gives her tight little ass a resounding smack. "You distracted me with all your sexiness, and I never packed a bag."

"I'm so sorry. You're right," she says eagerly. "I should definitely be punished."

"She sounds way too excited to be contrite," Michael says,

shifting in on my opposite side, a grin on his face. "She's even wiggling her ass for more."

Dani giggles because Doc is right. She's definitely arching her back to give Nathan better access.

"Now that deserves another smack," Nathan says, doing just that.

The sound of his palm connecting with her bare flesh has my dick throbbing, as does her reaction. She moans, deep and low, her adorable little laugh cutting off instantly.

"You like that, you naughty girl?" I growl.

She nods. "Yes. I'm such a bad girl, aren't I?"

"So bad," Nathan agrees. His eyes are dark as he runs his palm softly over the curve of her ass then gives her another light crack.

Dani likes Nathan's dominant style. Hell, she likes all our varying personalities, but in the bedroom she loves when Nathan goes full dom. Which I love to watch. "You're our naughty little plaything, aren't you?" I ask as I start walking again, entering Nathan's bedroom.

"Yes. You know you all can do anything you want to me. Anything." Her voice and expression shine with sincerity and love.

That level of trust makes my heart just about burst open with love for her. She's fucking amazing.

I glance over at Nathan, and he's paused in the middle of taking his pants down. He looks stricken by her words, nostrils flaring with emotion and desire. Dani's trust means everything to him because it's a level of intimacy he's never had with a woman.

With all of us.

I never have either. This relationship we have going is deeper than any I've had before, and nights like this give me something I didn't even know I needed.

"Oh, we're going to punish you, and then we're going to love on you all damn night," Doc says, leaning over and giving her a teasing kiss, his tongue dragging across her bottom lip.

When he eases back, he adds, "Put our sweet Cookie down, Crew. We need to decide what we're going to do to her."

I toss her down on the bed because that's the vibe she's clearly craving. It's not hard, but it makes a point. She's not getting gentle loving tonight, and we're all clearly on the same page about it.

"I know exactly what we're doing," Nathan says, kicking off his pants. "Take that top off, then all fours, Danielle," he orders. "And take your punishment like a good little slut."

"Excellent plan," Doc says, getting undressed and folding his clothes to deposit on the chair by the door.

I don't have his level of tidiness. I shuck, drop, and kick my pants to the corner.

Dani instantly obeys Nathan's command. The sight of her red hair tumbling down over her shoulders as she presents her ass for a spanking has me moving around to climb on the bed in front of her. When my hard cock is in front of her, she looks up at me from under her eyelashes.

"May I?" she asks.

"Hell, yeah. I've been waiting all day for this. Open your mouth."

Her lips, swollen from our kisses and her own tangy sweetness that Nathan kissed onto her from his own mouth, part readily for me right as Nathan shifts around the opposite side of the bed from Michael and slaps a crop into his hand.

Dani's eyes widen. She turns to see what the sound was right as I slip the head of my dick between her lips. I groan as the moist heat of her mouth covers my swollen tip.

"We have another gift for you," Nathan tells her. He slides the edge of it along his palm and whacks it on his flesh again in demonstration.

Goosebumps appear on Dani's back and arms as she flicks her tongue over my cock and watches Nathan intently.

The four of us had discussed introducing some toys into the bedroom because it's clear Dani wants to explore more, and we had a consensus on a few different options. One was spanking with a crop, which really seemed to intrigue Dani. Us guys had done a little online shopping together, teasing Dani about it for the last week.

I hadn't realized the package had arrived.

Seeing Nathan drag the black leather over the curve of Dani's peach has my balls tightening and my mouth going dry. Burying my fingers in her thick hair, I turn her head back to face my dick directly. I don't want her to know or anticipate when a blow might occur. "Look at me," I tell her. "Open nice and wide and take that dick like a good girl. Make me come."

She licks her lips and gives me a sweet sexy smile. Then she encloses her mouth over my cock and starts to take me deep. Except Nathan lands the crop on Dani right then and she jerks in shock, her lips tightening on me.

I groan. She moans around my cock.

Michael makes a sound of approval, reaching under Dani. "You need something else, baby?" he asks. "How about my finger?"

She nods and shifts her hips so her legs are spread wider, accepting his touch. With one hand still in her hair, I trace the other down the curve of her spine, watching goosebumps appear in the wake of my touch. "You like that?" I ask her. "You like Michael finger-fucking you while you suck my cock?"

Dani pulls back enough to breathe, "Yes. I love it. So much."

She does. She's rocking onto him and each time she shifts backward, she draws in her cheeks, sucking me in tighter with her slick warm mouth. My thighs are clenched as I enjoy the sensation of this woman—our woman—taking my dick like it's her job. A job she fucking loves.

"I love it too." Enough that I'm not sure how much longer I can last. Tension is rippling through all my muscles, my grip tightening on her hair, taking over the rhythm and fucking her mouth.

"What about you, Hughes?" Nathan asks, running the leather

crop down the backs of Dani's thighs. "Enjoying feeling that tight little pussy before it gets fucked?"

"Oh, yeah. I think she's nice and ready." Michael's voice is tight.

He wants inside her heat with more than his finger.

Dani is getting desperate. She's trembling, her skin flushed with color.

I'm so deep in her mouth that her eyes are watering, and she's pumping herself back onto Michael.

Nathan smacks her ass again and again, now in a steady rhythm, and after thirty seconds, she flies apart, writhing in her ecstasy.

The sight is so gorgeous, I can't hold out. "I'm coming," I warn her through gritted teeth, right before I fill her mouth with my own hot explosion.

My eyes drift close briefly, but then I force them open as I pull away, enjoying the view of my cum sliding down over her lips. She sucks in a shuddery breath then moans.

"More."

But Nathan is already rotating out to take my position. "Go for it, Hughes."

Michael doesn't hesitate. He shifts to the end of the bed and drives his dick into Dani from behind. She gives the most glorious cry of pleasure. I stand up on shaky legs and stand where Doc was previously, reaching out to tease at the tight little pebbles her nipples have hardened into.

Nathan eases himself into her mouth.

We're in total sync now, working together to take Dani to that place where she's a quivering mass of orgasm after orgasm, her moans drifting into each other, all our minds empty of any thoughts of anything other than the pleasure we share.

Michael's palms tighten on Dani's hips and he pauses briefly before he comes with a curse. Dani reaches up and squeezes the base of Nathan's shaft as she glances back at Michael and murmurs, "I love you."

His voice is tight. "I love you, too, Cookie."

Then she stares up at Nathan and tells him, "I love you."

He shudders and gives a low groan as he spills into her mouth. "I love you, too, Danielle."

I release her nipples and pet the back of her hair, sensing her exhaustion. "You good, babe? You want more?"

Her green eyes lock on mine. "I want you."

Giving my cock a couple of hard pulls to make sure it's hard enough—which it is, because watching her, there's no other option—I stalk to the end of the bed as Michael moves away, shaking his head in bemused satisfaction.

I'll never get tired of this. Of her. When I run my fingers across the curve of her backside, I indulge in drawing out the moment, teasing between her cheeks, and finding her swollen bud.

But Dani's having none of it.

"Please," she begs. "Crew. God, I need you."

"You heard the woman," Nathan says. "Give her what she needs."

That's all the encouragement I need.

Once I'm inside her, there's no going slow. I pound into her tight heat and tell her, "I fucking love you. I love you so much."

"I love you too, Crew."

Our orgasms blend together, while Nathan holds Danielle's head and Michael watches her expression intently.

Then we're all on the bed, holding Dani, petting her, spent and satisfied.

"I guess I really should pack," she says, rolling on her side with a grin. "We have an early start tomorrow."

"I'll pack for you," Michael offers.

"I'll buy you new clothes," Nathan says.

"I like you naked anyway," I tell her, brushing back an errant curl from her cheek.

"That will make quite the impression," she says dryly, her cheeks still pink from exertion.

"My parents already love you. And so do yours."

"We'll see when we get there."

I don't know fear. It's not a familiar feeling to me at all. Not on the ice, not in my personal life. I don't give a shit about spiders, or flying on airplanes, or standing on glass floors at high heights.

But Dani getting hurt?

Now that fucking scares me.

"What can go wrong? Besides, parents, especially moms, love me."

They do. I can charm a rattlesnake.

Then again, my overconfidence is arguably my weakness.

But I shove that thought aside and cuddle with my girl until she falls asleep sandwiched in between me and Michael, Nathan taking the outside.

Between the three of us, we can get her through anything.

Even Christmas.

CHAPTER 4
Nathan

I WANT TO BE PISSED.

Part of me is.

But a bigger part of me realizes that this is my own fault. I should have expected this.

You dumbass. You agreed that McNeill could be in charge of this.

And I will never really be able to explain why I thought letting Crew be in charge of our transportation for the three family Christmases that are going to take us from Illinois to Indiana and then back to Illinois was fine.

Maybe because the guy is a fucking professional athlete who travels in luxury all the time? Whether it's the private planes or the luxury buses the team uses, or the town car and SUV that we use when the four of us go out, or the damned sports car he personally drives, Crew McNeill knows expensive, comfortable, and good-looking modes of transport.

So, I gave Andrew the holiday off. Of course, I did. I'm not a monster. I'm not going to make the guy drive our asses around to these fucking Christmases. And when Crew said he knew the perfect thing for us to take on the road trip, I'd said fine.

Of course, Danielle is also to blame.

She wants to give Crew more responsibility. She wants me to

show that I trust him. Which, okay, is a little fair. But they'd proposed the idea of Crew being in charge of transportation while they'd been decorating Christmas cookies four days ago, and I'd been…distracted.

Because Crew and Danielle, of course, don't frost Christmas cookies like normal people.

Oh no. Hughes had baked five dozen cookies—for fuck's sake—and then Crew and Danielle had mixed up eight different colors of frosting, had at least six different decorating tips, and had bought at least ten different kinds of sprinkles.

And then Crew had turned it into naked cookie decorating.

And our Cookie had ended up with frosting and sprinkles all over her sweet body, and Crew had "needed" help eating her up.

That's when they'd sprung this idea on me.

So, no, I can't be blamed for thinking it was fine. Everything had been very fine at the moment.

Which is why I am now standing on the sidewalk outside my building in downtown Chicago, where I paid over ten million dollars for the penthouse, with my suitcase at my feet, staring at the enormous blue and white RV parked at the curb with Crew McNeill standing in the doorway with a huge grin.

"Let's go!" he calls to us. "Lori McNeill's brunch waits for no one!"

"Why are you driving Cousin Eddie's RV?" I demand.

Crew's face brightens even more, and he jumps from the top step to the sidewalk. "You know *Christmas Vacation* and Cousin Eddie?" He seems delighted.

I cross my arms. This RV looks almost exactly like the one from the iconic movie.

"I don't live under a rock," I tell him. For fuck's sake, I was a kid when that movie came out. Of course, I know it. He really does think I'm a stodgy old man. I love proving him wrong.

Crew is shaking his head as he approaches. "Every time I think you're just a jackass I have to put up with for the love of my life, you pull something out that makes me think you're actually a human being, Armstrong." He comes to stand beside me. He puts his hands on his hips, facing the RV. "Isn't it great?"

"This is the exact opposite of great, McNeill. There's no way we're taking that thing on this trip."

"Are you kidding?" he asks, looking at me aghast. "My dad is going to flip over this. He's going to quote so many lines from that movie, and he's going to want me to record him doing it in front of this thing! And I know Dani's dad is going to love it. Maybe Michael's too."

And what a fantastic way to remind me that I could be Danielle and Crew's father.

I scrub a hand over my face. Michael has taken Danielle's bag and stored it, so she comes to stand with us. She links her arm with mine, cuddling close. "My dad will get a kick out of this. He loves that movie."

"Where the fuck did you even get this?" I ask McNeill. I know I'm going to lose this argument.

I've lost more arguments since falling in love with this woman than in the rest of my adult life put together. I sigh.

"My buddy from college," Crew says. "His name is Eddie, and he's always dreamed of having this RV. He's a little sensitive about the fact that this is a 1971 Ford Condor rather than a 1972 like in the movie, but he repainted it and everything, and we assured him it's a really good replica. Even though this one doesn't have the rust and shit." Crew chuckles. "He was going to paint parts of it brown to look like it. We talked him out of it."

"Small miracles," I grumble.

"So I paid Eddie a couple thousand to let us borrow it to go to Indiana and everywhere this year," Crew says. "I want to make a good first impression."

I roll my eyes. Of course, McNeill would think this was a good first impression.

He claps me on the shoulder. "Let's get going. It's going to be slower going in this." He takes Danielle's hand and tugs her with him.

And he *paid* someone to use this thing? Jesus.

"Where would you like these, sir?"

I turn to find my doorman, Christopher, holding two of the biggest poinsettias he's ever seen. I know, because he told me so when they were delivered. The other doorman, Pete, is holding a third, awaiting my direction.

I sigh and then gesture toward the RV. "Inside. Somewhere."

"See?" Crew calls from the doorway of the monstrosity. "A regular SUV would have never had enough room for all of us, our suitcases, and those damned plants."

I'd decided to show up at each house with a poinsettia. So sue me.

"Not to mention, we're gonna need room to stuff Dani's stockings later," Crew says, giving our girl a big wink as he climbs into the driver's seat.

She giggles, and I frown. "What are you talking about?"

"Sex, Nate," Crew deadpans. "I'm talking about sex."

I take a deep breath, then blow it out. "You think we're having sex in this thing?"

"Well, we're not going to be able to at Dani's mom and dad's," Crew says as he starts the engine. "She gets kind of loud." He grins up into the rearview mirror at her. "And ball gags feel like a New Year's thing."

"Oh my God!" Danielle exclaims. But she's not protesting.

My dick gets a little hard. Dammit, these two teasing never fails to do that to me.

Or Hughes. He's leaned over, whispering something in Danielle's ear that has her flushing a deeper red. But smiling and nodding.

"You sittin' up front with me?" Crew asks me.

I'm just standing inside the doorway, not in the front or the back.

I glance at the passenger seat, then at the seats in back.

"Sit with me," Danielle says to me quickly.

She knows I'm grinding my teeth together over this whole

thing. She holds a hand out to me, and I instantly feel a little tension leave my shoulders.

"I'll sit up with Crew," Michael offers, standing and moving to the front.

I exhale and take his seat, linking my fingers with Danielle's.

"Don't worry," she says with a smile. "Lori makes a great brunch, and her mimosas are really strong."

I huff out a laugh. "I need more than a little champagne."

"Well, if those aren't enough, I know where the liquor cabinet is," she says.

That's right. She's been friends with his sister since college. Danielle has been to Crew's parents' house before.

Just as that thought occurs, Danielle's phone dings with a text. She reads it, grins, and calls, "Luna's waiting for us outside the shop."

Crew's sister—Danielle's best friend and business partner—is riding with us to their parents' house, where we'll leave her when we head to Indiana and Danielle's family's Christmas.

I take a deep breath. Let the family Christmas chaos begin.

CHAPTER 5
Michael

CREW AND LUNA MCNEILL grew up in the freaking *Home Alone* house.

That's my first thought as we pull up in front of the huge white house in the Chicago suburbs. There's no room in the driveway—it's already full of other vehicles and this crazy-assed RV we're driving takes up far more than its share of the room.

I have to grin though. The thing is hilarious.

It's very on-brand for Crew too. We're turning heads everywhere we go. And he's eating it up.

And hell, it's Christmas. We're bringing the *Christmas Vacation* RV to the *Home Alone* house for our own version of *Four Christmases*. And we've got our own personal Grinch along. I smirk as I glance at Nathan. I can't wait to see what other cliches we can mix in.

Luna leads the way up the walk to the front door adorned with one of the biggest Christmas wreaths I've ever seen. Lights strung from the eaves and over the manicured evergreen bushes on either side of the brick front steps that lead up to the door.

Nathan and I hang back as Crew slips an arm around Dani's waist and starts for the door.

Dani looks back at us. "What's wrong?"

"Nothing," I tell her quickly. "We're right behind you."

This is going to be a great stop. I glance at Nathan. For all of us, even though Nathan looks like he's approaching the door to the dentist's office with a broken crown and four cavities.

There are clearly a large number of people already inside based on the full driveway. Nathan's not a social butterfly, that's for sure. In social situations, Nathan Armstrong almost always has the upper hand. People interact with him because he has money and influence. Most parties or gatherings he attends, he's hosting. Which means he can choose who is invited, and he can choose when he leaves. If the boss leaves early, no one can say much about it.

Here it's a whole different thing.

For one, Lori McNeill, Crew's outgoing, perky, warm mother is in charge. And Nathan won't do a damned thing to make her unhappy. Not because she's bossy or bitchy, but because he likes her.

Nathan really likes Crew's mom.

We've met Lori and William McNeill a couple of times already. They, of course, come to games sometimes, and since Crew's big speech on the ice letting all of Chicagoland in on our relationship, Lori and William have been sitting with Nathan and Dani when they make it to games.

The first time we all met, Nathan hosted them in the owner's box before Crew and I had to be downstairs for pre-game stuff.

They were both wonderful.

William had shaken our hands with a sincere smile and had seemed unfazed by the fact that we were all openly dating the same woman. Together. We'd talked hockey, Crew's first season as a Racketeer, and how great Dani was. Topics all three of us were enthusiastic, knowledgeable, and in full agreement about.

Lori had hugged us both tightly, said she knows Crew can be a handful, and thanked us for putting up with him—though she said it with one hundred percent affection—and told us that our taste in women was impeccable.

The way she interacted with both Crew and Dani was full of love, support, and warmth, and for that alone, I loved her.

Just as Luna reaches the door it suddenly swings open, and her father steps out. "Welcome!"

Immediately four guys about Crew's age stumble out from behind him, nearly knocking him and Luna over, calling, "Sorry, Mr. McNeill" and "Hey, Luna!" as they nearly fall down the steps.

"Crew!"

"Is that your RV?"

"No way!"

Right behind them are two more, slightly younger guys, and another man who stops next to William.

Crew is grinning and has already followed the small herd of men past us and back to the RV.

Luna is on the top step hugging her dad, but I hear her say, "What a bunch of idiots."

I step up next to Dani, taking her hand.

William is laughing. "Those are hockey teammates of Crew's from high school," he explains to us. "We've always been good friends with their families, and they always come over for Christmas brunch. Their parents are all inside."

"That's not really the *Christmas Vacation* RV is it?" one of the younger guys still on the steps asks.

"A replica," I tell him. "But it's pretty close."

"Is it yours?" the kid asks me. Then he looks at Nathan.

"God, no," Nathan tells him.

I laugh. "Belongs to a friend of Crew's."

"That's hilarious." They both bound down the stairs to go check it out with the hockey players.

"That's Grant and James. Two of Crew's cousins," William tells us. "And this is my brother, Dave."

Luna rolls her eyes. "Yes, you two can go look at the crazy RV too." She's laughing as she nudges her father.

He grins. "Well, maybe just for a minute."

We stand back to let them both pass as well, watching them

join the group of guys checking the RV out from bumper to bumper and posing for selfies by it.

"We should get a big hose and find a bathrobe and pose like Cousin Eddie!" someone suggests.

Crew sticks his head out of the doorway. "Told ya', Nate!" he calls with a huge grin.

Nathan just sighs and shakes his head. But I know him well enough to see the smile he's fighting.

"I don't know how you put up with him all the time," Luna informs Dani.

Dani's smiling at Crew and his friends. "He's…adorable," she says with clear love in her tone and on her face.

"That's our line," I tell her, pinching her ass gently.

She giggles. "Well, his sister might not want to hear that when he acts like that—all playful and full of joy and like a big kid—it makes me want to tear his clothes off and climb him like a tree."

"Ugh," Luna groans. "His sister definitely does not want to hear that." She steps through the open door and calls, "Hey! We're here!"

"Oh! Hi! William just suddenly got up from the table and a bunch of the boys followed him out of the kitchen, and I had no idea what was going on. I'm so glad you're here!" Lori says, breezing into the foyer. "We've been waiting." Her gaze goes to the open door and the commotion at the curb. "Oh Lord, what are those idiots doing?"

Nathan actually chuckles at that. "It's a replica of the RV from *Christmas Vacation*."

She lifts a brow. "Crew's idea?"

"Yep."

"Figures."

She shakes her head, but she's grinning. "Well, come on. It might take them a bit to get over that, but there's no reason you can't be warm and have coffee in the meantime."

She moves behind me, pulls my coat from my shoulders, and then slips my scarf from around my neck.

Dani is laughing, watching. She's already handed her coat over to someone, and she's toeing her shoes off.

Nathan is also being helped out of his coat. He gives me a bewildered look. I just shrug and lean over to untie my dress shoes.

Once we are coatless and shoeless, Lori herds us into the kitchen.

The house smells like maple syrup and bacon, and as far as I'm concerned, that is a fantastic start to any event.

Lori's kitchen is magnificent. She clearly loves to entertain and designed the house with that in mind. The kitchen flows directly into the dining area, so the people currently seated around the huge dining table are able to visit with everyone milling about the kitchen, drinking coffee and mimosas.

She has two ovens, both of which are currently working, and a wide island covered with platters. Some are filled and some are waiting to be filled.

"Where can I help?" I ask.

She waves that away with a laugh. "Don't be silly. Everything is done. I just need to pull things from the oven."

"Great." I move toward the ovens, reaching for an oven mitt, but she stops me.

"No. Sit." She points to the four stools that are pulled up to the island. Luna and Dani are already perched on two of them, munching on fruit kabobs.

I expected that response, whereas at my mother's house, she'll be handing me an apron the moment I walk in and pointing me to whatever needs to be done next.

"Nathan."

His head comes up. He was looking at his phone.

"No phones during brunch. The coffee bar is right behind you. Help yourself," Lori says as she dons two oven mitts.

He actually looks sheepish as he tucks his phone into his pocket. "Sorry," he mumbles.

I chuckle as I move in next to him, checking out the coffee bar.

This little section of the kitchen is set up just for beverages. Mugs and glasses are in the glass-fronted cabinets above. The countertop has a coffee machine almost as elaborate as the one in Nathan's kitchen. It will provide everything from espresso to cappuccino to plain old black coffee. There is a plethora of coffee pod flavors displayed, as well as teas and cocoas. Underneath there's a refrigerator full of water, both plain and sparkling, juices, and sodas.

We both prepare a cup of coffee.

As Nathan's finishes brewing, a woman about Lori's age moves in next to us for a refill.

Or rather, a refill that acts as an excuse to come talk to us.

"Hi," she says with a smile, setting her cup under the spout. "I'm Melissa. I'm Lori's sister."

"Nice to meet you. I'm Michael Huges," I say. "This is Nathan Armstrong."

"I know. I've heard all about you both," she tells us with a smile. "It's so nice to meet Crew's boyfriends."

Nathan chokes on his coffee, and I press my lips together.

Before I can correct her, Melissa goes on, "Oh, don't worry, we've all known for a long time that Crew is bi-sexual."

Nathan coughs harder.

"And we're all fine with it. We're supportive. Allies. Whatever." Melissa frowns. "I feel like I'm messing this up. Is this not how to talk about it? I'm sorry." She sighs. "I've been reading and trying to say it all right. I'm just learning."

I give her a gentle smile and elbow Nathan. "I think it's wonderful that you're trying to learn because of your nephew. And I think you should talk to him about it. Ask him what terms and words he wants to use. And don't feel bad about talking with us. Every relationship is different, so we're all learning how ours is going to work too. It's still new. Nathan, Crew, and I are very good friends, who care a lot about each other."

She looks relieved, if still a little confused. "Okay, thank you. It really is nice to meet you."

"You too, Melissa," I say sincerely.

Crew, William, and everyone else swarm into the kitchen just then. The space definitely gets more cramped and louder.

Nathan and I move to the side, picking a spot along the wall between the kitchen and dining room to lean. Then we'll be here, but out of the way.

Nathan and I had agreed that while at the McNeill's we would let Crew and Dani have center stage, and we'll just hang out in the background.

But Lori is having none of that. The minute Nathan's back meets the wall where he clearly intends to lean for the next little bit, she is tugging him forward and pushing him onto the stool next to Dani at the island. Crew has already taken over the stool where Luna had been sitting. She's now next to her grandmother at the dining table.

There's one stool left at the center island, and I know before she even points to it that Lori intends it for me.

Dani is between Crew and Nathan, and she reaches over to put her hand on Nathan's thigh. He takes a deep breath. That's good. She'll keep him calm. Ish.

"Okay! Let's eat!" Lori calls. "It's buffet style, so come fill your plates, then find a place to sit! There's another big table set up in the living room!"

Within minutes, there's nowhere for us to go. There are people behind us, beside us, and in front of us as they encircle the island and all the food.

I'm from a big family, but this kitchen is *packed*.

Clearly, these are neighbors and friends of the McNeills, not just relatives. Though Lori is teasing and scolding the guys from Crew's old hockey team as if they are her sons.

The general mood in the room is jovial, affectionate, and warm.

I love it.

"Okay everyone," Lori says. "We want to welcome the newcomers to our family, too, before everyone scatters. This is

Danielle, Crew's girlfriend. And this is Nathan and Michael, Dani's other boyfriends."

All four of us stiffen. We are literally in the middle of the room, seated on stools where everyone can see us, and I guess we're just going to put that all out there.

"Okay, Mom," Crew says with a chuckle, running his hand over Dani's back.

Lori's eyes widen. "Oh my gosh, is that not how I'm supposed to introduce you?" Her gaze scans over all four of us. "Because I mean, you're not really his boyfriends. I mean, you're not sleeping together. I mean, I know you *sleep* together. But you're not really *sleeping together*." She shakes her head. "Unless you are. Which is great. That's completely fine with us. Of course."

Nathan has now swallowed coffee down the wrong pipe again, tried to breathe, and gotten more coffee in his lungs. I'm wracking my brain for the right thing to say here. Dani is bright red but trying very hard not to laugh. And Crew lost the fight with trying not to laugh two seconds in. If he was even trying not to in the first place.

Crew reaches over and slaps Nathan on the back. "Okay, so first, maybe I should point out that Armstrong is also my boss, and you all need to be at least a little cool."

Nathan thunks himself on the chest, shaking his head.

Finally, I say, "That is probably a fine way to introduce us, Lori. Though, I would say that Crew, Nathan, and I are good friends as well."

"I mean, you'd kind of have to be," a man leaning against the refrigerator says.

"Everyone, my uncle Tony," Crew says with an eye roll.

"I'm just saying, you see each other naked, right?" He doesn't seem to be poking at us or trying to embarrass anyone. He's just curious.

They all seem curious. It's… kind of nice. This is Crew's inner circle. Strangers on the internet aren't entitled to details about our private life, but these people maybe are. Not *all* the details, of course. But if they have basic questions about how our relationship works, that's fair.

"I've seen all of those guys naked multiple times, too," Crew says, gesturing with his fork at his ex-teammates. "And I've seen Jack Hayes and Blake Wilder naked a bunch of times too, but they're not my boyfriends." He digs back into the cinnamon roll he's eating.

"But you're going on dates together," Tony says.

"You mean going out to dinner, movies, concerts, hiking, shopping?" Crew asks. "Hell, Tony, you and I have been on a bunch of dates then."

Tony thinks about that. "I guess everyone is just assuming that it's more since there's sex involved."

"And no one really knows what goes on in our bedroom except the four of us," Crew says, lifting a shoulder and seeming much more concerned about getting icing on every bite of his cinnamon roll than he is about what people think of his sex life. He takes the last bite and looks up at his uncle. "People at work asking you?"

Tony nods. "Yeah. Some are dicks about it, but most are just curious. You know they follow you and are big fans. Guess they think they can ask questions since you're my nephew."

Crew nods and reaches for a second cinnamon roll. "I get it. Just tell them you saw us all at Christmas, and we seemed really happy." He glances down the island at the three of us. "Because we are." Then he looks at his uncle. "That's just vague enough it will drive them nuts, and it will mean they'll keep following us on social media."

"Yeah, I'll do that," Tony says, nodding.

"But you need a photo with the four of us," Crew adds. "So they believe you really saw us."

Tony smiles. "That's perfect."

"We're so happy that you're happy, baby," Lori tells Crew, scooping eggs onto his plate.

"Yeah, I mean, think of how awkward it would be if two of

you guys irritated the shit out of each other or something," Luna says, propping a hip against the island and grinning at us.

"Very awkward," Crew agrees. Then he winks at Nathan.

I think I'm the only one that hears Nathan's growl. But I know he's thinking up ways to mess with Crew later.

"I just want to know what exactly to say to three hot guys to get them to agree to all date you at the same time. Like in the same room together." This comes from a girl who has a shoulder propped against the wide arched doorway that leads into the living room.

She's young. Like really young.

She's obviously talking to Dani. "And talk slow," she adds. "I'm taking notes, and my friends want me to tell them everything."

"And that's my cousin, Hadley. Who is only sixteen," Crew says.

Now Dani chokes slightly. She swallows and says, "Well, I was going to give you some notes, but how about you call me in two or three years."

I'm proud of her for rolling with that and making it funny.

"How about we make it ten or twenty years?" a man calls.

"Her dad," Crew adds.

Everyone laughs at that. But we all also see Hadley motioning to Dani that they'll talk later.

"Yeah, if anybody's getting those tips, it's going to be me," Luna says. "I live with the girl and have to watch them all be gaga over each other on a daily basis."

That causes Lori to give us a brilliant smile.

"And that is the most important thing," she says. "You're all clearly together for the right reason. The rest works itself out."

"I don't know," another woman says. "No offense, but that sounds like a nightmare. One man was too much for me, and it took me twelve years to get rid of him. Having three at once? No, thank you."

I chuckle. "My sister said something similar," I say to her. "I suppose it very much depends on the four people in the relationship."

Dani is the one who nods and adds, "I never imagined being in a relationship like this. It's not about having three guys. It's *these* guys. I fell in love with my soul mate…it just happens that I have three."

That makes my chest tighten, and I can't resist the need to reach over and touch her. I squeeze her hand. She gives me a sweet smile. Nathan and Crew both have hands on her too. Just simple, loving, though possessive gestures. Nathan's hand is on her thigh, and Crew's hand is resting on the back of her neck.

People keep talking, and asking us questions like who takes care of the laundry, what about all the dishes, and do we really go everywhere together?

Answers—we all pitch in on basic laundry, though there is a laundry service Nathan likes and we all use sometimes, and Crew's "disgusting hockey stuff" (his mom's words) is handled by the team, we share with the dishes, and sometimes we all go out together, sometimes we take Dani on individual dates, and hell, sometimes it's just the guys when she's hanging out with Luna. We also all like alone time sometimes, so we have our own apartments. Correction, everyone but Crew likes alone time sometimes.

Finally, their curiosity has been satisfied, and the topic shifts to hockey, then eventually to other topics.

As we all climb into the RV several hours later, we collapse into our seats. Dani and Nathan in back, and Crew and me up front.

We take a collective deep breath.

Dani looks at each of us. "Well, that was… lovely."

Crew chuckles. "Could've been worse. Sorry for the third degree. That was even a little more intense than I expected."

"It was fine," I jump in before Nathan can say anything. "They were curious, and maybe a little awkward in how they worded things, but it came from a place of love and interest in your life.

No one was judgmental, harsh, or mean. And I hope we helped them answer the questions they're getting because people know they know you."

"I agree," Dani says. "They were a little more in our faces than I expected, but it really did seem well-intentioned. And honestly, if it was one of my cousins in this position and I ran into her at Christmas brunch, I might ask questions too."

Crew and I laugh.

Then we all turn and look at Nathan.

He looks a little shell-shocked.

Dani leans into him, running her hand up and down his arm. "Are you okay? You were really quiet today."

He nods. "I was really happy to have you all around…with me…today."

Dani looks pleasantly surprised. "Really?"

"You all handled all of that so well."

"Sorry it was a little awkward at times, Boss," Crew says, sincerely.

"I expect that. Ninety-nine percent of my interactions with other humans are awkward and awful," Nathan says.

Dani squeezes his arm and cuddles closer to him. "Not true."

"It wasn't today," he agrees. "I got to let you all handle the people, and I got to eat stuffed French toast and quiche, and drink some of the best coffee I've had outside of my apartment. That's all I had to do. I got to just sit and be quiet and know I had people there to handle things even better than I could." He shakes his head. "I never get to do that. I never get to feel that way."

Crew looks like Nathan just announced that he was giving Crew his Lamborghini—shocked, and delighted.

"Well, fuck Nate, wait 'til you taste my mom's pot roast. You'll want to go over there every Sunday. There aren't nearly the number of people, and Lori can keep up a conversation without anyone else contributing more than a 'yep' every once in a while."

But instead of saying something sarcastic, Nathan nods. "Sounds great. I love pot roast."

Crew turns wide eyes on me. "How many mimosas did he have?"

I laugh and look back at Dani and Nathan. She's gazing up at him like she just fell even more in love with him. And like she's thinking the same thing I am—Nathan Armstrong needs a little mothering, and I think Lori McNeill would be a good one to do it. Even if she's only about seven years older than him.

Nathan looks down at her, then over at me, and then finally, his gaze lands on Crew.

"Your family is wonderful," he says.

Crew grins. "Thanks." He keeps his eyes on Nathan when he says, "I have pretty great taste in people."

Then Crew puts the RV into drive, and we pull away from the McNeill house.

CHAPTER 6
Dani

WITH EVERY MILE the RV heads south, I feel the joy and warmth of the McNeill's welcome fading as anxiety creeps in.

The hugs, smiles, and casual acceptance Lori and William extended to me, and to Michael and Nathan, are not going to be present with my parents. The conversation I had on the phone with them where I explained I was bringing not one, but three, boyfriends home for Christmas went over exactly as I'd expected. They were absolutely stunned.

My parents aren't heavy communicators anyway, and they certainly don't yell, but their silence is painful. On that call there was a whole lot of dead air. Like the kind where you actually think your connection has dropped because there's just… nothing.

Crew is driving the RV and Nathan is sitting in the passenger seat next to him because he doesn't trust Crew driving. They're talking hockey, with lots of phrases being thrown around that I don't understand as a newbie hockey fan. It's me and Michael in the back, watching It's a Wonderful Life on his laptop, his arm around me.

"Hey," he says softly as the movie ends. "What's going on?"

"Hmm?" I look up at him. His dark brown eyes are filled with concern. I lean into his chest and breathe in Michael's scent. He always smells like leather and books and sandalwood. It never fails to both calm me down and turn me on.

He strokes the back of his palm down my cheek. "You're getting more and more tense by the minute, and you've sighed about fifteen times. Are you nervous about seeing your parents?"

Of course, Michael is tuned into my emotions. He always seems to know how I'm feeling. I pull back a little so I can see him better, biting my lip. "Yes. I'm starting to think this was a mistake. Not even Nathan's enormous poinsettia is going to make up for the fact that instead of bringing one guy home, I'm bringing three. I don't think my parents even knew that could be a possibility. I have officially blown their minds and not in a good way."

"Are you afraid they're judging you or that they won't want a relationship with you anymore?"

"Both." I almost choke on the word. "Not that they said anything like that, but they just didn't say anything at all."

"Yet they agreed we could visit."

I nod, but he doesn't understand. My parents would agree to a potluck with Satan rather than risk being seen as rude.

Michael sets his laptop down on the table and turns to face me more directly. He studies me. "I'm worried about you. Your face is all flushed and your shoulders are up to your ears."

He tries to rub my shoulders and I realize he's right. They're locked.

"I just…"

I don't finish the sentence because I'm not sure what I even want to say. I feel like I can't breathe.

"Crew," Michael calls out. "Can you find a rest stop or an exit to pull over?"

"Bathroom break already?" Crew asks. "Can't you hold it? I worked really hard on letting all the speed demons pass and not allowing myself to get boxed in by semi trucks. I found a sweet spot, and I'm making good time in this bad boy right now."

"It can't wait," Michael says firmly. "Dani's upset."

"What's wrong?" Nathan asks, his head whipping around.

I shake my head, my throat tight. "I don't think visiting my parents is a good idea. They didn't react well to our relationship at all. We probably should get a hotel tonight."

"Why would we get a hotel when we have this awesome RV to sleep in," Crew jokes, glancing at me in the rearview mirror. His eyes display concern his casual tone doesn't convey. He's already exiting the highway.

Nathan is up and out of his seat, striding to the bench and taking the seat beside me opposite of Michael. "Danielle, why didn't you tell us you were worried? I don't like that you've been bottling all this up." He takes my hand. "You can tell us anything, sweetheart."

Taking a deep breath, I try to relax my shoulders while I try to find the words to convey how I'm feeling. "I know that. I do. But I'm hurt and embarrassed, and I didn't want any of you to feel bad about that. But avoiding the problem makes me feel like I just set you all up accidentally to be in the most awkward Christmas Eve dinner ever." I groan, closing my eyes briefly.

"Literally fifty percent of my Christmas Eve dinners have been awkward," Nathan says. "Maybe sixty. Don't worry about me. I can handle angry parents. I'm a pretentious asshole, remember?" He gives me a smile and brushes my lips with a kiss.

The RV turns into a parking lot of a fast-food restaurant and Crew puts it in park.

"You're not an asshole," I tell him. "Quite the opposite. And my parents weren't angry. They were just... silent. Like they didn't say anything at all. They acted like I never told them."

"So, they'll be polite but disapproving," Michael guesses.

"Exactly."

"No mother disapproves of me," Crew says as he unbuckles his seat belt and strolls down the aisle. "I told you. Moms dig me."

I want to believe him. "You are pretty charming," I tell him. "Especially when you're trying to get what you want."

He leans on the table in front of us and reaches out to tuck my hair behind my ear. "Which is you. That's what I want for Christmas, and I don't mind if your parents don't welcome us with open arms. I'm good at filling the silence."

"You definitely are," Nathan says wryly.

That makes me chuckle softly in spite of my nerves.

They're already making me feel better. My throat doesn't feel like it's being squeezed by a boa constrictor.

"I deal with people in awkward situations all the time," Michael says. "Players who don't want to hear they're on the bench, social media, team owners who think they have a medical degree and know when a player should be on the ice." He side-eyes Nathan.

Nathan ignores that. "Exactly. I've kissed ass with charitable donors, I've negotiated with hostile coaches, and I've had to explain about my grandfather's prognosis over and fucking over. Silence can be dealt with."

"I promise there won't be any silence," Crew says with a wink.

"They didn't forbid us to visit, so maybe they just need to see us all together to wrap their heads around our relationship," Michael suggests. "We'll make the best of it, Cookie."

God, these guys. They take such good care of me. In their very different ways. Michael is calm and soothing, Crew always makes me laugh, and Nathan's confidence reassures me every single time.

"I love you so much," I say, glancing between all three as tears well up in my eyes. "I'm the luckiest girl ever."

They all chime in with a chorus of "I love yous" and each man gives me a kiss.

My toes curl. "Maybe we should get a hotel anyway," I suggest, tilting my head flirtatiously. "Last night was so long ago."

"Your turn to drive, Nate," Crew says, tossing him the keys before dropping down on his knees in front of me. "I know the perfect stress reliever, Dani." He eases my knees apart.

I shiver, eager to be pleasured, eager to be distracted. "What is it?" I ask teasingly, even as I ease my skirt up my thighs, exposing my pussy for his view. Since the RV can act as a home, Crew put forth, and the guys all agreed, that the no panties at home rule applies here.

Nathan curses, but he stalks to the front and gets in the driver's seat as Crew starts to kiss the inside of my thighs. "You'd better hope I don't hit a pothole, McNeill."

Crew flicks his tongue over my clit before easing into my tight channel.

I groan as he strokes in and out. Michael takes my chin and turns me toward him for a deep, lingering kiss that mimics Crew's tongue in my pussy. I'm suddenly on fire.

The RV rumbles to life and the motion of the vehicle only adds to the sensation of spiraling out from my core, both men penetrating me with their tongues, until I'm flying. The orgasm sweeps over me, and I shudder into Michael's mouth, fingers in Crew's long hair with a white-knuckle grip.

I tremble before my whole body goes slack with relief, and I sink into Michael's arms.

"Better?" he murmurs as he nuzzles my ear.

I nod. "Much."

Crew pulls back and wipes his mouth, a look of pure satisfaction on his face.

But then he tries to stand up right as we turn out of the parking lot. I reach out to stop him when it's clear he's going to hit his head. "Crew, wa—

It's too late. He cracks his head on the underside of the table.

"Fuck!"

"Are you okay?" I bend down, reaching out to massage his skull and check for injuries.

He shakes his head like a dog after a swim. "I'm fine. I've been hit a lot harder than that." He crawls out from under the table.

"Is he okay?" I ask Michael, needing a physician's reassurance.

"He's fine." But he looks toward the front of the RV. "Though maybe that turn was taken a little too hard, Armstrong."

"I'm getting used to this beast," Nathan says. "There's a learning curve."

Our whole relationship has a learning curve. I need to remember that. There is for the four of us. We're all still learning how to maneuver this dynamic, so of course there will be questions and concerns for my parents as well. But they love me and want the best for me, so hopefully this will turn out better than I'm expecting.

And if not, we may be sleeping in the RV tonight because it's probably too late to find a hotel anywhere given it's Christmas Eve and we're in rural Indiana.

Knowing my guys, they'll make even that special. The RV is already bursting with poinsettias and presents, and the colorful string of holiday lights Crew hung.

Nathan has even turned on Christmas music.

"Let me make you a Christmas cocktail," Michael says, getting up and heading to the kitchenette.

Michael makes great craft cocktails. He's as creative in the kitchen as he is in bed.

"Something with cinnamon," he adds. "And whipped cream." He tosses me a sensual smile.

Oh, yeah. Everything is going to be very merry tonight. I'm the happiest I've ever been in my entire life and these guys are the reason.

"I would love lots and lots of whipped cream, thank you."

"That's our good girl," Crew says, bending over to kiss me hard. "Good girls get lots of presents, Dani. Keep that in mind when I tell you to get on your knees and suck my cock later."

"Why wait until later?"

CHAPTER 7
Crew

I SHOULD HAVE BRUSHED *my teeth.*

That's the thought that pops into my head as we stand on the doorstep to the Larkin's tidy house.

I can still taste Dani's sweet tangy arousal on my tongue.

How the hell am I going to hug her mother with pussy breath?

Then I realize there probably won't be any hug offered given what Dani said earlier about their reaction to our relationship. And the fact that the four of us are standing here freezing our asses off on the stoop waiting to be let in. Why the hell does Dani need to wait for the door to be answered to the house she grew up in?

Impulsively, and because I'm freezing in my suit with no overcoat, I try the door. It's locked. My family would never lock the front door on a holiday. It also would never occur to me to do anything other than just walk right in, and my whole extended family is the same way. Open door policy. But maybe my family is unusual.

I look over at Hughes. He gives me a "what the fuck?" look so clearly, he agrees with me. Nathan doesn't look like he thinks anything of it, but he wasn't raised in the middle-class suburbs like me and Doc. He probably had a butler as a kid and a high-tech security system with cameras. Locked doors would be normal when you have expensive possessions.

The Larkins could be hiding anything behind the door of the tiny bungalow, but I doubt it's bags of cash.

Dani rings the bell again.

"What are your parents' names again?" I ask for the third time because fuck it, I'm nervous, and when I'm nervous information goes in my ear and out the other.

I hate being rattled. I'm not good at it. It's out of character for me so that when tension does sneak in, I don't know what to do with my energy. I'm tapping my palms on my thighs and bouncing on the balls of my feet, wishing I hadn't changed. Per Dani's request we had all put on suits in the RV prior to arrival, but my tie feels like it's strangling me. I also have the sudden concern that I should have gotten a haircut. Or paid more attention shaving.

Or not eaten out their daughter half an hour ago.

"Nate, check my breath," I murmur to him when Dani doesn't even answer my question. She's texting on her phone.

Nathan gives me a withering stare. "Crew, go fuck yourself."

"Now that's the holiday spirit," I tell him. I do a breath check in my palm. "Dani, their names?"

"Kevin and Mary," Dani finally says, obviously distracted as she leans back to peer through the picture window. "But don't call them that unless they give you permission. They're very traditional, I've told you that. It's Mr. and Mrs. Larkin."

Now my tie is really too tight. I tug at it. She sounds annoyed with me. I know she's not. She's just stressed about seeing her parents, but I still feel a little called out. My own tension escalates. I'm both freezing my balls off and sweating bullets all at once. I reach out and brush my hand over the snow dusting the hedges to the right of the stoop. I slap my damp palm on the back of my neck to cool my skin.

"Why is the house so quiet?" Nathan asks. "What time is it? Didn't you say dinner is at six, and we should arrive by five?"

She nods. "Yes. I don't know why there aren't cars in the driveway either. There should be ten people here."

"It's five-fifteen," Michael says, frowning.

What unnerves me further is that Doc sounds unnerved. I don't like that. He's no alarmist.

"Should we—

Whatever he's about to say gets cut off by the door finally opening.

"Oh, hello!" A woman around sixty gives us a startled look as she takes the four of us in before focusing on her daughter. "Danielle, I wasn't expecting you."

What the hell?

As she envelopes Dani in a hug, I exchange looks with the guys.

Dani sounds flustered and upset. "What do you mean you're not expecting me? I told you multiple times I would be here on Christmas Eve!"

"Didn't you get my email this morning?" Mary asks, her green eyes, so much like Dani's, widening. "Your aunt has the flu, so we canceled our usual family dinner. I assumed that meant you wouldn't be coming." Mary Larkin looks over her daughter's shoulder. "Or that *they* wouldn't be coming."

The disdain for us guys rings through loud and clear. Dani's mom does not want us here.

This is awkward.

And for once in my life, I'm actually speechless.

Nathan, who has people dislike him on a regular basis, looks undeterred. "You must be Mary, Danielle's mom. I'm Nathan Armstrong." He puts his hand out. "It's a pleasure to meet the woman who raised our Danielle."

Our Danielle. He definitely did that on purpose, and I appreciate him making it clear right off the rip we are not shying away from the truth of our relationship. He also completely ignored that we're not supposed to use her mother's first name unless given permission.

Mary's eyebrows shoot up, but she automatically takes Nathan's hand and limply shakes it. "It's Nathan?"

He nods. "Yes."

"Nice to meet you," she says faintly, pulling her hand back.

Dani looks stricken and on the verge of tears. "An email?" she demands. "Mom, I wasn't checking my email on Christmas Eve! And while I'm sorry that Aunt Linda is sick, what about everyone else? Grandma, Uncle Pete, Aunt Jessica, my cousins?"

"They couldn't make it," her mom says with a vague wave of her hand, sounding guilty as hell.

The implication of that is also loud and clear. She doesn't want to explain to her family why Dani has brought three men home for Christmas.

Her mother won't look Dani in the eye but instead lands her gaze on Michael, who immediately puts his own hand out.

"I'm Doctor Michael Hughes, Mrs. Larkin," Michael says. "It's so nice to meet you. Dani has such great memories of growing up here with you and your husband and all your family traditions. She's been looking forward to seeing you again all week. She really misses you."

Michael never introduces himself as a doctor. That's a nice touch to butter up Mrs. Larkin. I approve. She seems to approve as well. He gets something that seems like a genuine smile out of her.

"We miss her too." After shaking Michael's hand, she reaches out and strokes Dani's hair off of her face. "She hardly ever comes to visit anymore."

"Maybe because you leave her standing on the doorstep when it's twenty degrees," I joke.

It just slips out. Because I'm cold and nervous and fuck it, why are we still squashed up against each other on a stoop when I see a gas fireplace and can smell burnt caramel a few feet away inside? Nathan's got one of those damn poinsettias on the walkway behind us, and it's basically up my ass.

"Oh, God," Dani murmurs, raising her hand to her forehead and massaging her temples.

"Crew," Michael says, giving a small head shake at me to indicate that was the wrong thing to say.

"It's a joke. I'm obviously kidding." And we're obviously all still standing on the doorstep. "Dani definitely misses you, Mary, but the bookshop keeps her busy."

As does being sexually satisfied by her boyfriends. That takes a *lot* of time.

"But we should try to get down here more often." I hold my hand out. "I'm Crew. McNeill. The hockey player. And Dani's favorite." I give Mary a wink.

She leaves me hanging and doesn't take my hand. "Call me Mrs. Larkin."

Ouch.

Mrs. Larkin turns and opens the door wider. "Come in, everyone. Kevin! Dani is here!"

"Seriously?" Nathan murmurs to me as we enter the house.

"You called her Mary," I protest under my breath. "How come I'm the one in trouble?" I tug at my tie again. I wear a tie all the damn time. I don't know why it's bothering me so much today.

"Take your shoes off," Mrs. Larkin commands. "This carpet is new."

I jump a little and immediately toe my shoes off.

"Mom, this carpet was new when I was in high school. You got it for my graduation party." Dani shakes her head. "Do whatever you feel comfortable with, guys."

But Nathan and Michael are already ditching their shoes as well. Danielle's mom is petite and seems sweet, but she also gives off a distinct fuck-around-and-find-out vibe.

Nathan hands Mary the poinsettia. "This is for you. Merry Christmas. Thank you for having us."

This damn plant is so large that Mary's hands sag under the weight of it, and the leaves cover half of her face. Also, it's a stupid thing to say because she doesn't want us here, but does anyone say anything about that to Nate? Nope. But I don't want to upset Dani anymore than she already clearly is, so I let it slide.

I can't see her face, but I hear Mary's voice drift out from behind foliage. "Oh, my goodness. Thank you. This is just lovely, Nathan. How thoughtful of you."

Nathan smiles in triumph at me, which adds to my irritation.

"What did you say, Mary?" A man's voice calls out from somewhere in the house. "And close the door. You're letting all the heat out."

The house is not an open-concept floor plan. We're huddled in a tiny living room, and there are doors and stairs everywhere. I feel very large and crowded next to Nate and Doc. And the poinsettia. Dani is peeling off her coat and draping it over the banister leading to the second floor.

"Dani's here!"

"Is she by herself, or did she bring her gang of men?"

I cough into my fist, overcome by the urge to laugh. Damn, I'm trying my best to be mature, but it's getting harder and harder. This is so bad, it's almost funny.

"Kevin!" Mary gasps, sounding horrified. "We're all in the living room."

She puts the poinsettia down on an end table, and I can see how much Dani looks like her mother. She has the same red hair, though tinged with gray, and she blushes as easily as her daughter. Her cheeks are tinged pink now.

Dani is also blushing. Michael is bending over, murmuring something in her ear. When her father, a tall, thin man, enters the room, Nathan takes the lead and strides over to him confidently, introducing himself with a firm handshake. "Nathan Armstrong. It's a pleasure." He hands Kevin a bottle of bourbon. "We brought this for you. Danielle told us you're a bourbon man."

That seems to warm Dani's father up a tad. He shakes Nathan's hand and takes the bottle. Then he studies Nathan. "How old are you?" he asks, looking skeptical.

"Dad, stop!" Dani looks like she wants the floor to open up

and swallow her whole. Her cheeks are almost as red as the pretty cocktail dress she has on.

I feel defensive on Nate's behalf. We're the only ones who get to harass him about his age. "Younger than he looks," I quip.

That draws Kevin's attention straight to me. His eyes narrow. "You're Luna's little brother."

"Yes. Crew McNeill. It's nice to finally meet you, sir."

"Oh, I know all about you," is his only comment.

I have no idea what that means. Probably nothing good, but I nod. "Excellent."

I don't know why I say that. It's just what comes out of my mouth, and now that it has, I'm at a loss for what else to say. But the awkward silence is immediately filled by Nathan speaking.

"I'm forty-one," Nathan says, circling back to Kevin's question, like he's determined to just push through this and appease Dani's parents in any way he can. "I have no criminal history, not even a parking ticket. I've never been married, so no angry ex-wives, and I don't have any children. I'm square on my taxes, and I have more money than Oprah."

Now I do give a chuckle. I can't help it. It's clear I'm not the only nervous one here because that was a hard sell.

"More money than Oprah, you say? Then you could have at least brought me two bottles of bourbon." But the corner of Kevin's mouth turns up slightly. Then he turns and puts his hand out to Michael. "And you're the only age-appropriate one here, nice to meet you."

Michael, our unflappable designated dad, looks actually sheepish. "It's a pleasure, sir."

"Michael is a doctor," Mary says, smiling in approval.

"Excellent." Kevin claps Michael on the shoulder. "Maybe you can talk Mary out of looking up all her ailments online. Every road leads to cancer on those damn sites."

"They are definitely a slippery slope," Michael agrees.

Kevin gestures for Michael to come further into the house. "Well, come on in, Doc."

Mary follows, wrapping her arm around Dani.

I'm left standing there with Nathan, a little stunned by how unimpressed Dani's parents are with me. I admit it. I'm used to the star hockey player treatment. This sucks.

Nathan is rubbing his jaw.

I feel his pain. This sucks for him too. Michael is the runaway favorite with his damn medical degree and birth date.

"There were supposed to be ten more people here?" Nathan murmurs, looking around the living room. "I've been in elevators bigger than this one."

"Bigger than Oprah's elevator?" I ask, unbuttoning my jacket.

Nathan actually sighs. I'm not sure I've ever heard him sigh. Now I really feel for him. I'm not the only one sticking my foot in my mouth.

"I don't know why I said that," Nathan said. "Fucking ridiculous."

He sounds grumpy, which reassures me that he'll rebound. Grumpy Nathan is normal. Sad Nathan is not. Seeing him down is like an alternative universe I don't want to live in.

"It's okay, buddy," I tell him with a grin. "We've all had Oprah envy at one point or another."

Nathan actually cracks a smile. "Shut up, McNeill."

That's the Nate I know. I feel better.

"At least you and me are in this together," I add. "They're treating me like I'm in high school, and I snuck in Dani's window."

"You may be doing that later. There's no way they're letting us share a room with her, you know that, right?"

He's totally right. I make a face. "Damn. The holidays are hard."

Mary pops her head back into the room. "What are you two doing? Come on now. I opened a bottle of wine."

I'm going to need that whole bottle myself at this rate.

"Can I do anything to help you?" I ask, striving for politeness as I move forward.

"I can open a bottle of wine," she says. "Even if it isn't some fancy wine."

I'm going to just assume that second comment was directed at Nathan. "Yes, ma'am."

Then she disappears again behind some other wall, and Dani appears in her place. "I'm so sorry," she whispers. "I'm so embarrassed. Please, come in," she said, holding her hand out.

She's fighting back tears. It's like a punch in the gut.

I go right to her, take her hand, and give it a squeeze. "It's all good. Don't worry, sweetheart. We're big boys. We're fine. We can take a little heat. Haven't you seen me on the ice? I get shit talk on a regular basis."

She kisses my cheek, which settles my nerves. "You are definitely a big boy," she murmurs flirtatiously in my ear.

I take a deep breath and vow to pull it together as she moves past me to Nathan. We need to be supportive of Dani, like we promised her. She warned us her parents were not on board with our relationship, so none of this should be a real shock. We just have to stay calm, be polite, and show them we're just normal people in a nontraditional relationship.

"Are you okay?" she asks Nathan. "You seem nervous."

"What gave it away?" he asks wryly. "The verbal background check I gave your father?"

Dani laughs softly and reaches up to give him a kiss. "I love you and your lack of a criminal history."

"Jesus. I really said that." He shakes his head. "I promise that was my only outburst of the night."

"I'd hold off on that promise," Dani says with a smile. "We have a lot of Christmas Eve to go."

But once we move past the tiny kitchen, where Mary has Michael slicing cheese and plating crackers and grapes with it, and into the family room, Kevin is cracking open the bourbon.

"Grab some glasses there behind you," he tells me. "Let's try this."

As I turn and stare in confusion at a cabinet that is stuffed to the gills with glassware, gravy bowls, and platters, I debate what might be considered a bourbon glass. I'm more of a beer guy, and even then, I don't drink that often. It doesn't fit into my hockey schedule.

"Sorry for the miscommunication," Kevin is saying.

I open the cabinet. There are tumblers with Niagara Falls on them. I start to reach for them because the only other thing I see to drink out of is a couple of mason jars and tea cups. Without warning, Nathan's hand reaches past mine and passes over a platter with a turkey on it, to glasses buried way in the back.

"Not a problem," Nathan says, his back to Kevin. "The holidays can get chaotic." He gives me a look of solidarity and hands me two glasses. He takes a third out for himself.

Relieved, I turn and nod, handing a glass to Kevin. "We're just happy to be here."

"Mary should have just called and told Dani we weren't doing a big thing this year instead of sending an email."

"Kevin, don't blame me," Mary says from the kitchen, which is mere steps away. "We discussed it together."

"It would have been great if you had discussed it with me," Dani says, pouring herself a glass of wine in the kitchen. "Because now you've made Nathan, Michael, and Crew feel completely unwelcome, and I feel like you don't trust me to know how to live my life."

"I'm not trying to offend any of you," Mary protests. "I just need time to process this. It completely caught me off guard, and the idea of meeting all of you for the first time with a whole bunch of family here was just overwhelming to me."

That was fair, yet her avoidance has us all sitting here feeling awkward as fuck. Worst of all, she's upset Dani.

"We understand," Michael says, handing a glass of wine to Mary. "It is a lot to process. I think if we can all just spend some time and get to know each other you'll see that we care about Dani and want to make her happy."

"Since we're clearing the air, I'm just going to come out with it," Kevin says. "No PDA in my house."

"What's PDA?" I ask blankly. I'm still holding my empty glass. Kevin is already sipping from his now-filled glass.

"Public display of affection," Nathan tells me.

It takes me a second. Then I realize that means we can't touch Dani in front of her parents.

"You all are adults, and you're going to do what you want to do," Kevin says. "Just not in my house."

I stare at the bourbon, mentally willing it to jump out of the bottle on the table next to Kevin and into my glass. I'm getting nervous that I'm going to say something I might regret. Again.

"And we trust you to know how you want to live your life," Mary assures Dani, sitting down in an easy chair with her glass of wine and patting the arm for Dani to perch on it. "It's just like mentally rearranging everything I've always assumed. Do you understand, sweetheart?"

Dani nods and leans against the arm. "I do. All I'm asking is that instead of avoiding the situation, you at least try to get to know these guys. They're good men. Great men."

Kevin rubs his temples. "Danielle. You know all we want is for you to be happy."

"That's all we want, too, Kevin," Nathan says firmly. "And I think we've done a damn good job of it."

He sounds a little defensive, but Dani smiles warmly at him. "You have," she says simply. "I'm the happiest I've ever been."

"Danielle is our miracle baby," Mary says. "We were married fifteen years before she came along."

That explains a thing or two, and I can appreciate where they're coming from, but I don't get them not supporting their daughter's choices.

"Mom, I was your miracle baby. I'm an adult now."

"Of course, you are." Mary massages Dani's back. "I just always thought there would be a wedding, grandbabies…" Her voice trembles without warning.

I almost joke that I'll get Dani pregnant if they want, but I stop myself in the nick of time. Because I'm fucking mature, damn it.

"If I want those things, I can still have those things," Dani says, sounding exasperated yet sympathetic. "But if I do, it's because I want them, not because you want them. It's my life," she adds gently.

Michael puts a platter of cheese and crackers down in front of us. I stuff a piece of cheese into my mouth, which is a mistake since my glass is still empty.

Does Dani want marriage and kids? We've never discussed it. I don't even know what that would look like for Cookie & Co. Communication is going to be key. Glancing over at Michael, I can see he's thinking the same thing as me. If our relationship continues the way it has, we should talk about what the future holds in store. The idea of having kids now terrifies me. I'm not ready for it. At all.

This is a good reminder that we need to address all that.

But that's for later. Right now, I need to figure out how to swallow this damn cheese. I clear my throat a little, and nothing happens. I try again, but nothing. My face feels hot.

Dani's mom jumps up. "Crew, are you choking?"

I shake my head, coughing. I hold my hand up to indicate I'm okay.

"Why doesn't he have a drink?" Mary demands of her husband. "He's choking, Kevin."

"Oh, shit, sorry," Kevin says. To his credit, he seems to realize for the first time that he hasn't poured me and Nathan any bourbon.

Even as I'm wheezing and holding my glass out to accept a pour, I understand that Dani's parents got blindsided by our relationship. They had a picture of what their daughter's life would be like, and they need time to regain their equilibrium. But if they can say there is no PDA in their house, I'm setting down a rule or two of my own to protect our girl.

Mary comes over to me, and now it's my back she's rubbing.

Kevin has splashed bourbon in my glass, and I take it all back in one swallow. It gets the cheese down, but it burns like hell. I cough into my hand as Mary reassuringly pats me.

"It's okay, just breathe," she tells me.

Her touch feels very maternal, and I appreciate it. I nod. "Thank you."

"Let me get you some water," Dani says, going to the kitchen.

I clear my throat again and turn back to Mary, then to Kevin. "Look. I just want the both of you to know that we—me, Nathan, and Michael—all love your daughter, and we will never intentionally hurt her. We'll do everything in our power to keep her safe and happy, just like you did her whole childhood. We're not asking you to understand our relationship, because, hell, sometimes I don't even understand it myself. But I want you to stop and ask yourself if you want to be responsible for making your daughter cry. Because she almost did today because of the way you handled this visit." Kevin is sitting stiffly, listening. A glance back at Mary shows she looks stricken and pale. "And I know how much you love your daughter and that you never want to see Dani cry, let alone be the reason for it."

Mary has tears in her own eyes. "No, I never, ever want that," she says softly.

Michael nods in approval. "Well said, Crew. We just ask you both to keep an open mind and get to know us all individually and together, that's all."

"I lied," Nathan says. "I did get a parking ticket once, in college, when I parked in the bus lane. Since we're being honest."

His delivery is classic, dry-as-hell Nate, but it breaks the tension. Dani laughs, which makes Mary giggle. Me and Michael grin.

Dani hands me a glass of water and tells her parents, "And we will respect the no PDA rule."

Yet even as she says it, she glances back at me and shoots me a look so hot that I clear my throat again. There could be something to this no-touching rule. It will amp up the tension and make me want her even more. Stolen kisses here and there, a hand on her thigh under the table, brushing against her in the hallway—this could be a fun game. I may even have to sneak her into the RV later.

In the meantime, we're all waiting to hear what Dani's father's response will be.

Kevin just slaps his hands on his thighs, nods, and stands up. "Welp. Let's order some Chinese food for dinner. And let Mary show you baby pictures of Dani."

CHAPTER 8
Nathan

AFTER DINNER, Crew offers to help Mary with the dishes. I almost laugh out loud. He helps with dishes at home but never jumps up and practically sprints to the kitchen to do it. He's now chattering away with Mary as she rinses plates and glasses and hands them over to him to load into the dishwasher. He is *desperate* to make her like him.

I'm not sure talking at her like a five-year-old hopped up on candy and Santa's-coming-tomorrow adrenaline is the way to do it.

I actually feel myself grin, even as I shake my head. I'm sitting at the table with Danielle between me and Michael. There are scrapbooks spread out, and she's telling us stories about the photos and what seems to be every piece of artwork she created from the time she could hold a crayon or glue stick to the time she left home.

Her parents have clearly doted on her since the day she was born. I've never seen this many photos and mementos of one person's life.

It's sweet and touching, and clearly she's enjoying all the memories.

No matter how cool or judgmental they've been, I like and

respect Kevin and Mary Larkin simply because they created Danielle and have loved her so fucking much.

Have they smothered her a little? Made assumptions about her? Not always listened to her? Sure. But after being in their home for even a couple of hours, there's no question that they love her.

Michael's arm is over the back of Danielle's chair, not really touching her, per her mother's rules, but his index finger drags back and forth over the back of her neck now that Mary isn't looking.

I lean in. "Where's your dad?"

Danielle looks up and glances around the kitchen.

"He's probably out in the garage. It's kind of his man cave."

I nod and start to get up.

"Where are you going?" She looks worried.

"I'm just going to go talk to him for a minute."

She grabs the sleeve of my shirt. "You don't have to. He'll be fine."

I look at her with one eyebrow up. "I am going to talk to him, Danielle." I wasn't asking her permission. "Trust me."

Her teeth sink into her bottom lip as she studies my face, clearly trying to figure out if this is a good idea. I reach up and tug her lip free with my thumb. I haven't touched her all night. We've all been good about that. But it's difficult. At home, we touch freely. I didn't even realize how much until I had to keep my hands to myself.

It's not even sexual energy. I just want to caress her cheek or pull her against my chest for a hug.

I was never a touchy-feely guy before I met Danielle. I was definitely not a hugger.

Now I need a hug as much as she does.

"It will be fine," I tell her. I meet Michael's eyes. He gives me a little nod, which I interpret to mean that he'll make sure our girl is fine in here.

I start to straighten again and turn toward the garage door.

Now she catches my back belt loop. "Nathan—"

I turn back. Her mother's back is still to us, so I lean in, grasp Danielle's chin between my finger and thumb, and say low but firmly, "I'm respecting your mother's rules right now, but the no touching won't last. Do you really want the first touch from me to be a smack to your ass?"

She sucks in a little breath, and her pupils dilate.

And I know that my dirty girl is thinking that, yes, actually, she would very much like that first touch to be a smack to her pretty little ass.

I smirk, squeeze her chin, then let her go. "I'll be back."

She doesn't try to stop me again.

I go to the garage door and open it slowly. "Mr. Larkin?"

The overhead lights are all on. The far side of the garage has a pickup parked in it, but the half closest to me has a piece of brown carpet lying on the cement floor along with a recliner, a loveseat, a mini-fridge, and a TV sitting on top of an old dresser. He's in the recliner, clicking through channels, so I feel better that I'm not interrupting him by coming out here to talk to him.

He looks over. "Nathan."

I step down onto the first step and close the door behind me. "May I join you?"

Kevin aims the remote at the TV and turns it off. "I have a feeling you're only asking to be polite. I think you plan on staying no matter what I say."

I incline my head in agreement. I tuck my hands into my dress slacks. We all lost our jackets an hour ago. My shirtsleeves are rolled up, but while Crew's tie is God knows where, mine is still around my neck, though loose. I'm used to being dressed up like this all day long.

I'm also used to having difficult conversations and facing people who don't like me and with whom I'm at odds. But at this moment, I'm uncomfortable. This is Kevin's turf. And he is not an opponent. He is the father of the woman I love. And dammit, if we're not going to be friends or even get along, we need to at least have an understanding.

"I just wanted the chance to tell you a few things," I say.

Kevin sighs, then gestures toward the loveseat. "I'm sure your office is nicer than this."

I shake my head. "I'm much more focused on the words in meetings than I am on the furnishings."

"If someone had ever told me that I'd be sitting down to talk with the billionaire owner of a hockey team in my garage, I would've told them they were nuts," Kevin says, sitting back in his recliner. "If that person had told me that that same man would be banging my daughter, I probably would've punched him."

I take a seat on the loveseat, perching on the edge and resting my forearms on my thighs, linking my fingers. I take a breath and work on keeping my temper in check. "I appreciate you getting right to the point. I do want to make a quick, very important correction, though. I am not 'banging' your daughter. That would imply that we were having meaningless sex. I am very much in love with her."

"But you're sleeping with her."

Kevin is in his early sixties. He's roughly twenty years my senior. We're about the same number of years apart as Crew and me. And as Danielle and me.

And Kevin is going to have to get over that. Like I did.

"Yes, your daughter sleeps in my bed most nights."

"I don't need details," Kevin says, holding up a hand.

"Nor was I going to give you any more."

Kevin shifts in his chair. He won't make eye contact. "You have to understand that this is an awkward position for a father."

"Actually, Kevin, with all due respect, you're only feeling awkward because you're focusing on one aspect of our relationship. And I feel it's very important that you understand the big picture."

He meets my gaze now.

"Your daughter is an amazing woman. You've known her for

twenty-four years. I find it hard to believe that you're surprised that other people realize how incredible she is. And I am a very intelligent man. As is Dr. Hughes. As is, as much as it sometimes pains me to admit it, Crew McNeill. There is no way that any of us could have met and spent even five minutes with your daughter and not fallen completely in love with her."

Kevin frowns. But he doesn't argue with me about how wonderful Danielle is. That's a point in his favor.

"Most people don't fall in love with *three* people," he mutters.

"That might be true," I acknowledge. "Or our society says it's strange and not acceptable to do that, so they resist and repress their feelings. Fortunately, I met an amazing woman and two remarkable men who changed *my* mind about that."

Kevin's frown deepens, but I continue. "I can be a real bastard, Mr. Larkin. I have spent a lot of time with men who can be real bastards. I can be cold, unyielding, and unconcerned about other people's feelings and problems. But Danielle didn't care about any of that. Her light and love came into my life, regardless of all that."

I take a breath. "And Michael and Crew have been nothing but patient, and open, and accepting. They are two of the best men I've ever met, and they're the best friends I've ever had. I was helpless to resist being involved with any of them. As someone who has had very little family and love in my life, I can't believe they put up with me, to be honest. I'm the lucky one to be included. And even though it hasn't been very long, I am smart enough to understand what I have, and there is nothing—" I meet his gaze directly, making sure he's paying attention "—*nothing* that will keep me from being with them."

Kevin finally takes a deep breath and blows it out. "I...respect that."

"Do you?"

He nods. "Even if I don't completely understand it, and it might take some time to get used to this whole idea, I..." He clears his throat. "I have to admit that Danielle seems very happy."

I nod. "She is. *Very* happy. And I can promise you that she always will be."

"You better."

"And I respect that," I tell him sincerely. I lean in. "But I'm going to be honest and tell you that there will be times I'll mess up. I'll fall short of being the man Danielle truly deserves."

Kevin frowns but doesn't say anything.

"But when that happens," I continue. "Michael and Crew will be there to call me out and make me step up again. Just like when they fall short, I'll be there. Danielle will never want for anything. She'll never be alone. She'll never be unprotected." I take a breath. "Mr. Larkin, I would burn the world down for your daughter. Then Crew would pick her up and carry her across the ashes, and Michael would rebuild it to be everything she ever wanted."

He's watching me now with a mix of surprise and confusion and what I can only call hope. He wants this to be true.

"Thank you, Nathan," he finally says. "Danielle has always been our…treasure. We've definitely had our ideas about how we thought her life would go, but, at the end of the day, we want her to be happy and…loved."

"She is absolutely, most definitely that," I say.

"Then…fine."

I nod. But then I add, "And I need to be clear about one more thing."

"All right."

"We will protect her from everything, and *everyone*, that could possibly hurt her." I pause, to be sure my point lands. "And that includes you and Mary."

He frowns again, but he doesn't say anything.

"If coming here, or seeing you, is painful for her, upsets her, or makes her sad, you won't see her."

Kevin is looking at me, and I know he understands that I'm serious.

"We want her to be happy too, Nathan," he finally says. "We love her very much too."

"Then this will be great," I say, giving him a nod. I stand from the loveseat and extend my hand. "I want you to feel free to call me any time you have any questions or concerns."

He leans forward and takes it. "I appreciate that. But…I don't know that I'll have any concerns."

That's a great answer. "And I look forward to…the next holiday." I say it with just enough uncertainty that he chuckles.

"Easter. We usually have the family over for Easter dinner."

Easter. Well, that gives me a few months off from all the family togetherness.

Except, freaking Crew's birthday is in February, and I have a feeling the guy thinks his birthday should be a big deal, with a lot of people fawning all over him. As if that doesn't happen pretty much every third day as it is.

But as I head back into the house, I find I'm not dreading that.

I bet Lori McNeill makes a hell of a birthday cake.

And who knows, maybe by then we'll invite Kevin and Mary to join the party.

CHAPTER 9
Dani

NATHAN STARES at the air mattress with his hands on his hips. "You can't be serious." His voice is grim. "I'm supposed to share that inflated piece of rubber with Hughes?"

I giggle. After the afternoon and evening of tensions I've had, I'm exhausted, relieved, and ready to collapse on the twin bed in my childhood bedroom and sink into sleep. "It's not that big of a deal, is it?"

"Uh, yes, it is," Nathan says, bending down to push on the mattress. "What's the weight limit on this thing?"

Michael is already neatly folding his jacket and putting it on the chest of drawers that still houses the clothes I left behind when I went to college. I imagine it's stuffed with skinny jeans and graphic T-shirts, my high school staples.

"I have no idea, but I'm sure it's more than the two of you combined." I reach behind my neck, and undo my necklace, and roll my neck to release the muscle strain.

It was a (mostly) successful evening considering how it started.

The guys were amazing. Michael, as usual, was a rock of stability and reason, making hot chocolate with my mother post-Chinese food and directing conversation all night with innocuous topics like food delivery services, my childhood love of books, and our family lake vacations, all designed to make everyone feel comfortable. He even answered a bunch of Mom's medical questions about Dad's high blood pressure with patience.

Michael starts unbuttoning his dress shirt, but he holds out his hand for my necklace to place it on the dresser. His fingertips brush mine, and he gives me a warm smile. "I love you," he says.

I lean forward and give him a soft kiss. "Thank you for being you tonight."

"I wouldn't be anywhere else than here with you."

"At least one of you feels that way," I say, nodding my head in Nathan's direction.

He's now lying on the air mattress, fully clothed, turning left and right to test it.

"I wouldn't be anywhere else either," Nathan says. "Well, maybe a Four Seasons right at this moment *after* dinner with your parents, but only if you were there too." He looks up at me. "I'm trying really hard. I didn't say a word when your father called me a trust fund kid."

I instantly feel sympathetic. He is trying hard, even if he's being a bit of a grump right now. He's earned the right. "I know, sweetheart," I say, bending down and squeezing his arm. "I love you, and I appreciate how much you're trying."

Nathan isn't used to family dynamics in general, let alone my parents side-eyeing him all night. He's also used to being in control, and meeting all of our families makes him feel very out of control, which is why he walked in and gave a speech designed to ward off criticism. It was his way of trying to direct the situation.

He's learning that it only really works in the bedroom.

It's not easy for him, and it makes me love him even more.

"I will sleep on the air mattress for you," he says. "Because I know it was a huge concession for your parents to allow us all to be here. I'll take it as a compliment that they're letting me be in the same room as you." A smile plays over his face. "Unlike Crew."

I'm sure my father is enjoying the idea of these two grown, *big* men trying to sleep on this mattress. There's no way anyone expects them to get any rest. When my dad relegated Crew to the couch, he told Crew he was young, and his back could handle it. "I suspect he thinks Crew is impulsive and might try to fool around."

Nathan reaches out and slides a palm down my calf. "Little does he know I'm planning to do dirty things to you the minute this house seems quiet."

That makes me laugh. "Behave yourself. It's pretty clear that my mother's concerns and reservations about our relationship are because she's worried about what other people will think, and she's worried I won't have a traditional wedding and family life. I think my father is just horrified that this forces him to admit that I have sex."

Nathan sobers. "Your father loves you very much," he says. "I respect that he's concerned. They only want what's best for you. But I was very clear that the three of us are what's best for you."

I look down at him, my heart swelling. "Really?"

"Really."

"The *three* of you?"

The corner of his mouth tips up. "Yep. All three of us. I even called Crew intelligent."

Michael snorts. "Wow. That was quite the talk."

Nathan nods. "It was. One of the most important I've probably ever had. I've never talked to a father about how much I love his daughter. Or told him that *he* also needs to treat her right."

I gasp. "You didn't say that."

Nathan frowns. "Of course, I did. I won't have people making you feel the way you did today. Even if they are your parents."

"Nathan…"

He props himself up on one elbow. "Danielle," he says gently, but firmly. "One of my jobs is to protect you. Kevin and I came to an understanding."

"Thank you, Nathan," Michael says. He's even frowning. "I'm glad you took care of that."

I look back and forth between them. My father seemed fine when he'd come back in from the garage about fifteen minutes after Nathan had gone out to talk to him. In fact, he'd seemed great. And he'd kissed me on the top of the head and told me he loved me before I came upstairs to bed.

Wow. I don't know what to do with these men.

Finally, I say to Nathan, "Okay. Now take your clothes off."

Nathan's eyebrows shoot up. "Hell, yeah. I didn't expect you to agree." He immediately starts unbuttoning his shirt.

"No, I mean, get comfortable so you can sleep. So we can all sleep."

Michael is in his briefs. He sits on the air mattress.

Nathan rolls to the side from the shift in weight. "Damn, Hughes, how much did you eat this week? Too many holiday cookies."

"The only cookie I ate was Dani." He lays down with a sigh.

I slide my dress off, and Nathan gives a growl of approval. Then, before I can react, he's off the air mattress, earning a curse from Michael, and he's pushing me down on the twin bed in my bra and panties.

"Nathan, we can't," I protest, though it's weak.

"I'm getting in bed with you. I can't sleep if I'm not touching you."

"Nathan, we won't fit," I protest, though I'm secretly delighted he needs me to sleep well.

He lays down next to me and nuzzles my neck. "You're smiling. You want me to cuddle with you."

Maybe I'm not-so-secretly delighted. He can see right through me. "I never said I don't want you to cuddle with me. I said we won't fit. Which we don't." He's squished so close against me, I can barely breathe.

"Why are you wearing panties?" he asks, running a finger

over the front of my lace underwear. "We have a no-panties rule, remember?"

I shiver, squeezing my thighs together at the instant flare of arousal. "We're not at home."

I turn on my side toward the wall to get more room. It feels like one or both of us is going to topple off the bed and onto the air mattress. I settle the curve of my butt into his crotch, which causes him to groan in frustration.

He shifts around, and I see the screen from his phone light up out of the corner of my eye.

Now Michael groans too, but for a whole different reason. "What are you doing? Put your phone away, damn it."

"I'm buying us a house here in Franklin," Nathan says. "I can't do this every time we visit Kevin and Mary."

I try to roll over, but I'm wedged against the wall. But I can see enough that a row of houses is sliding by as he scrolls down on his phone. "What? Nathan, that's totally unnecessary."

He takes my hand and puts it on his hard cock. "Babe, it is one hundred percent necessary. Look, I already found one. Three bedrooms, two and a half baths, for... wait, that can't be right. It says it's only two hundred thousand. I'm buying this thing right now. Let me call my guy. Unless we want acreage. Do we want acreage? This one is half a million, but it's got a barn too."

The phone disappears from his hand.

"What the fuck?" Nathan demands. "Give me my phone back, Hughes."

Michael is standing next to the bed, Nathan's phone in his hand. "You are not contacting anyone at eleven o'clock on Christmas Eve to buy a house. Or look at a house. Or even talk about a house." He slaps the phone down on the dresser, picks up his folded pants, and shakes them out.

"He'll answer," Nathan says. "He's fine."

"I'm sure he will answer," Michael tells him. "That's not the point. Don't be an asshole. Cookie, come on."

"What? Where are we going?"

"To the RV so you can actually get some sleep."

"If you're going to the RV, I'm going too," Nathan says.

"And why the hell would we need a barn?" Michael demands. "You've let the holidays get to you, man."

The holidays might be getting to Michael, too, because he's more irritated than I would expect. But he's right. We definitely do not need a barn.

The whole situation makes me want to giggle. I realize I've been absentmindedly massaging Nathan's cock, which is now even harder. "I wouldn't mind going to the RV. But only if we wake up Crew and take him too. And we have to be quiet."

I think we all need a stress reliever after today.

Crew deserves some attention from me as well. He definitely seemed to be a little dismissed by my parents, and I'm not sure why other than his age. But he took it on the chin, and I want him to know how much I appreciate it.

How much I appreciate all of them.

Nathan gets up and promptly stubs his toe on the edge of the bed. "Motherfucker. Ow."

"You heard the woman," Michael says, sounding amused now. "Be quiet."

Nathan holds his hand out silently, glaring at Michael.

Michael passes him his phone back. He's completely dressed again. "And Cookie, we need to have a conversation tomorrow about this bedroom and all your DIY framed photos, obviously printed off the internet. I had no idea you were such a Harry Styles fan."

"One D for life," I say.

Then I look at both of them and start laughing.

Michael gets it. He starts laughing, too. "Liar," he tells me. "Three is your lucky number."

Nathan doesn't laugh. "I don't get it."

Which makes me laugh even harder. "You don't know who Harry Styles is, do you?"

"No, because I'm not a teenage girl in 2018."

CHAPTER 10
Michael

I'M TRULY FEELING like a kid on Christmas Eve as we sneak down the hallway past Kevin and Mary's bedroom door, down the steps, and past the Christmas tree in the living room.

Crew's not on the couch, but I have a pretty good idea where he is.

We don't even bother to grab our coats on our way out the front door. Dani's only got a hoodie and some old sweatpants on, along with some slippers she found in her closet. I sweep her up in my arms on the porch, and she's giggling as we jog down the front walk to the RV.

Nate knocks on the door, then tries the latch. It's unlocked, and he pulls it open just as Crew appears in the doorway.

His hair is sticking up, and he's in only his boxers. They're all black except for the panel in the front right over his dick that has a bright red wrapped gift in the center and says *Stop Staring At My Package* in big white letters.

"What's going on?" he asks.

It doesn't seem like we woke him, and I wonder if he was having trouble sleeping too.

He focuses on Dani in my arms. "Is she okay?"

Nathan pushes him back and climbs into the RV. "No. None of

us are fine. Move."

"What's wrong?" Crew looks concerned even as he backs up.

"We haven't touched each other for hours," I say, swinging Dani's feet to the floor and pulling the door shut behind us.

"And there's an air mattress on the floor in her bedroom," Nate bitches.

Crew laughs at that. "I couldn't even cut it on the couch."

"You're all spoiled," Dani says, looking at us all with amusement and love.

"Yes," I agree. "And now we're going to remind you that *you* are spoiled and that no touching rules are bullshit."

"Such bullshit," Crew agrees, reaching for Dani. But he has to reach around Nathan to get to her, and there's not much space.

It's an RV full of four adults, three of whom are big men.

Crew's already got the thing warmed up and doing whatever RVs do overnight when people sleep inside them. I can admit that camping isn't something I've done, and I have no idea how RVs work, especially RVs that are fifty years old.

But it's clear Eddie didn't just restore the exterior of this one. While the exterior could double on the set of *Christmas Vacation*, the interior did *not* look like this in the seventies. It's cramped because it's a damned RV and there are four of us, but it's definitely been modernized, and the back bedroom area was gutted and redone. There's a double bed back there now, but it's not even a queen-sized mattress. There's not room for much else, but at least there's that.

And up here in the main area behind the driver's and passenger's seats, where the table, kitchenette, and eating bench are, we can at least all stand, though we're essentially in a single-file line.

Nathan elbows Crew. "I know that hard-on isn't for me, but I'd appreciate not having it pressed against my ass, McNeill."

Crew grins. "Trust me, Boss, I have about a dozen places I can think of where I'd rather put it too."

"A *dozen*?" Dani asks. "Do tell."

I feel some of my own stress melting away as our dynamic

starts shifting back to normal and our girl is clearly feeling a little flirty.

I'm behind her, so I move in, my hands on her hips, moving her forward to press into Nathan. What we all need is some sweaty, naked time where we are all firmly in our usual roles. We need to remember that no matter what is happening around us, no matter what other people may come in and out of the outer circle around us, the four of us are at the center and the same, always.

Nathan's hands settle on her hips, and I run my hands up and down her arms. "So, we're going to have to be creative," I tell them. "There's not a lot of space in here."

"I don't want a lot of space," Dani says, one hand on Nathan's chest as she lifts an arm to loop it around my neck.

"We've had too fucking much space today," Nathan growls, his hands sliding up under her sweatshirt, stroking her sides.

He leans in and takes her mouth in a deep kiss. She arches close.

Crew reaches around, clearly not caring what Nathan can feel. He squeezes Dani's hip, and she moans.

I lean in, my knee knocking against the 'kitchen' counter. Nathan tries to move to give Crew some room to get closer, but his head knocks against the cabinets over the bench seat.

"Fuck," he mutters, pulling back and staring at her with heat. "If you won't let me buy a house, we're at least getting a goddamned hotel room." He reaches for his phone again.

"*No.*" I stop him, pressing Dani closer to him again. "You don't need to call anyone to fix this. *You* just need to take care of our girl."

We just need to be us. Right here and now. Where we're at. We all need to know that we can do that no matter what's going on around us.

Nathan needs to take control and boss her around. Hell, he needs to direct this whole thing. He's been out of control the entire day, and I know that's eating at him.

Crew needs to play with her and just let go and be himself without worrying about her mother thinking he's too young and immature.

And I need to treat her like our princess.

Nathan's jaw tightens. His eyes are still on Dani, but I know he hears me.

"Okay," he finally agrees.

"No, it's fine," Dani says, stroking his face. "This is weird, I know. There's not enough room in here. Let's just go back to the bed, and we can just–"

"Take your clothes off, Danielle," Nathan interrupts. His voice is low and firm, and his expression says there will be no arguing.

But this is Danielle.

Probably the only person on the planet who can push Nathan Armstrong and not suffer dire consequences.

Of course, it helps that she likes his punishments.

"Nathan, you've been so great today. I know you're tired and frustrated. I'm sorry today was so much. I know my parents were a lot. I knew this would be…difficult. Let's just sleep tonight. You don't have to 'take care of me' any other way."

Nathan growls. "Danielle."

She hesitates. I squeeze her sides. "Yeah?" she asks quietly. Clearly, she knows Nathan has reached a breaking point.

"Take your fucking clothes off," he orders.

I decide to be helpful, and I sweep her hoodie up over her head and toss it toward the front of the RV. I unhook Dani's bra and toss it up front as well. I cup her breasts from behind, playing with her nipples as Nathan watches. She presses her ass back against me, almost instinctively.

Nathan takes a deep breath, seeming to relax. "I don't want you to think right now, Danielle," he tells her, cupping her face and dragging his thumb over her lower lip. "I don't want you to worry or think about how any of us are feeling or how anyone else is feeling. This is about how *you* feel and getting you out of that pretty head."

I nod. Exactly. We need to help her forget about all the things she's been worrying about trying to mediate between her parents and the three of us. We just need her in this moment with us.

And all of us concentrating on her, our very favorite subject in the entire world, will get all of us out of our heads.

I put my mouth against her ear. "We need you, Cookie. Let us lose ourselves in you."

She shivers, and her head drops back against my shoulder. "Oh, yes, please."

Crew adjusts himself behind Nathan. "I just need to hear one time, '*Crew, this RV was a great fucking idea after all. I apologize for ever doubting you.*' That's it. Just once."

"Crew," Nathan says.

"Yeah, Boss?"

"Get Danielle naked."

Nathan moves to the side.

Crew grins and slides past him to stand in front of Dani. "Okay, he can say it later. After we fuck your beautiful brains out."

She laughs softly. He hooks his fingers in the top of her sweatpants and panties and strips them down her legs, kneeling to pull them and her slippers out of the way, then tossing them toward the front seats.

He starts kissing up her thigh, and I pinch her nipples harder. She moans, and her fingers tangle in Crew's hair.

He starts to lift one of her thighs to his shoulder, but Nathan stops him.

"No. Not like this."

Crew runs his hand up and down her thigh, and I kiss her neck.

"Then what?" Crew asks Nathan, looking up at Dani.

"I'm going to give you part of your Christmas present, McNeill," Nathan tells him.

Crew's eyebrows arch, and his gaze settles on Dani's pussy. "I'm in."

"Bring her back here." Nathan starts for the back of the RV, where the bedroom is.

Crew rises, slowly, dragging his mouth up Dani's body as he goes. He kisses her deeply, then takes her hand. "The Boss needs us in back."

"Whatever you say," she tells him."

Crew gives her a wink and tugs her down the very short hallway. I follow, watching her sweet ass as she walks. The energy is definitely feeling familiar.

Nathan is on the bed, sitting with his back against the wall at the head of the mattress. Crew stops behind Dani at the foot of the bed, and I stand at the side. There's just enough room for us to stand. There's *not* enough room for all of us on that mattress, though. I lean back against the narrow built-in countertop. There's maybe an extra inch of space above my head back here.

"Come here," Nathan says, holding his hand out to Danielle.

Nathan and I are still fully dressed, and Crew's in his boxers, while she doesn't have a stitch on.

She crawls up to join Nathan. I can't help but reach out and run a hand over her ass. The advantage of a small mattress and no space around it is that she's within reach no matter where she goes in this bedroom.

Nathan pulls her into his lap but turns her so her back is against his chest, facing us.

He spreads her thighs, hooking her feet over the outside of his calves.

Crew and I both groan.

"Loving my gift, Nate," Crew says, running his hand over his cock through his boxers.

Nathan runs his hands over Dani's body, cupping her breasts, tugging on her nipples, and then skimming his hands down her body to her thighs. He runs his middle finger over her center, making her gasp as he rubs over her clit, then he holds her open with two fingers.

"Jesus," Crew mutters, squeezing the front of his boxers.

"Danielle, tell Crew how many points he's scored this season and what his shooting percent is."

"Um..." She wets her lips and then focuses on Crew. "Thirty-seven goals and twenty-one point seven percent. Which is really good." She gives him a sweet smile.

Then Nathan dips a finger inside her, and her smile drops as she moans.

"Very good," he tells her.

Crew's eyes are wide. "You're learning my stats, Dani?" His hand rubs up and down his cock.

She nods. "Nathan's teaching me what they all mean and what yours–"

Nathan slides his finger deep, and she breaks off as she gasps. His mouth is against her ear. "How many games has Crew played?" He pumps his finger in and out, and she grabs his thighs.

"Um..." Her eyes drift shut.

Nathan's finger stops. "Danielle, answer the question."

Her eyes open and she focuses on Crew. "Um... games," she says, as if reminding herself of the question. "Forty-one. You haven't missed a game this season."

Crew nods. He actually looks touched. And incredibly turned on. "Right. That's right, sweetheart."

Nathan continues moving his finger in and out of her pussy. "So, Crew, you get to decide...do you want to hear our pretty girl recite all of your stats that she's learned just for you? Or..." He adds a second finger, and her head falls back against his chest as she moans. "...do you want to eat this sweet pussy so well that our dirty little slut can't think of anything but coming all over your face?"

Crew groans, his head falling forward. "So as long as she can remember my stats, I'm not doing a good enough job?" he asks. But he's already moving into place. Crew gets on his stomach between her thighs. Nathan even pulls her legs wider for him.

"Yep," Nathan says, looking smug. "You can have one or the

other. Your favorite fan knowing all of your numbers...or your sweet slut screaming your name."

Crew licks Dani's inner thigh. "There's only two numbers Dani needs to care about right now. How many orgasms she's going to have and how many inches of cock she can take."

"*Crew*," Dani groans.

"Move your fucking hand, Nathan," Crew mutters, his hands gripping Dani's knees.

Nathan complies. He lifts his hand to her mouth, sliding the fingers that were just in her pussy between her lips.

She sucks, and my cock pulses at the site.

Then Crew licks over her clit, and she cries out.

Nathan takes both breasts in hand again, tugging and pinching her nipples. Crew works her pussy with his tongue and mouth, and she's soon writhing between them.

"What's Crew's average time on ice?" Nathan asks her.

Her head moves back and forth. "I um..."

He lets go of her nipples and moves his hand to the base of her throat, tipping her head back. "Answer me, Danielle," he says firmly. "Crew's average time on ice."

She swallows, but I can see that Nathan is applying gentle pressure.

"Twenty...twenty-two..."

Crew is still licking at her clit, and now he adds a finger. She lifts her hips slightly, but Nathan puts his mouth against her ear. "Answer. Me."

"Twenty-two minutes, nine seconds," she gasps.

Nathan smirks, then kisses her neck. "Come on, McNeill, I thought you were good at this."

"You're an asshole," Crew says. But he grins up at them. "But...I'm going to reward you *so* well for knowing that, sweet girl."

She's breathing fast, but she says, "You've had forty-three assists."

Crew growls and lowers his head, sucking on her clit hard as he thrusts two fingers deep.

She cries out, and he doesn't let up.

"What's his PIM?" Nathan asks as she starts to lift her hips closer to Crew's mouth.

"Ask her how many hat tricks I've had, you dick," Crew says.

Nathan actually chuckles. Hell, I do too. Instead of asking about Crew's league-leading, very impressive five hat tricks for the season, Nathan's asking about his time in the penalty box.

"I don't..." Dani shakes her head. "I mean, I know it. But I can't...remember."

Then Crew does something–it's hard to see exactly what from my vantage point–that takes her up and over the edge with a loud, "Oh my God, Crew!"

He kisses his way up to her belly, slowly removing his fingers. Then he shifts up to kiss her.

When he leans back, she says, still breathless, "Five. You've had five hat tricks this season."

He grins and kisses her again. "My very good fucking girl."

"And twenty minutes in the box," Nathan mutters.

"Come here," Crew says to Dani, ignoring Nathan. He pulls her down the mattress until she's fully underneath him. He kisses her deeply, running his hands up and down her body, just pressing her into the mattress for a moment.

"Fuck her," Nathan orders.

Crew reaches down and lowers his boxers, freeing his cock. He lines up with Dani's entrance and thrusts.

She gasps his name again, wrapping her legs around him.

He pounds into her. "Jesus, God, you feel good," he says against her neck.

"Yes, oh, yes," she agrees, her fingers digging into his back.

"There's no room for us to take you together, so you'll have to be an extra good slut tonight and keep those legs open until we're all done with you," Nathan tells her, brushing her hair back from her head as Crew fucks her.

She moans, and Crew's rhythm picks up.

"Fuck, I can't hold on," he says through gritted teeth. "Dani... Jesus, Dani."

"Fill me up, Crew," she tells him. "Just let go."

And he does. He comes with a muttered curse, pumping his hips a few more times before he stops, dropping his forehead to hers. "Dammit, girl, you destroy me every time."

She runs her hands through his hair. "I love you, Crew."

"I love you too, Dani girl."

He kisses her, and Nathan says, "Get off her."

Crew lifts his head, laughing. "Next." He winks at her. "What a good dirty girl, just laying here, taking us one after another."

A little shiver goes through her that says she loves all of that.

"She's not just going to lay there," Nathan says. "Hands and knees, Danielle."

Crew whistles and moves off of her and the bed, pulling his boxers back up. "Fuck, yes."

She rolls to her stomach.

"Head towards me," Nathan says. "I want to see your gorgeous face while you take Hughes's cock."

A shaft of heat stabs me in the gut. I immediately straighten.

Dani looks over at me. She gives me a smile that makes my cock absolutely ache. "Be gentle with me, Dr. Hughes."

"I don't think you're worn out at all," I tell her, pulling my shirt over my head and shoving my pants off. I kick my shoes and pants to the side and reach for her, running a big hand over her ass.

"I'm feeling *very energized*," she tells me. She licks her lips. "I might be able to come up with some more hockey statistics, in fact."

"Oh really." I run my hand over her ass, and dip down between her legs. She's hot and sticky. I dip a thick finger into her pussy, and then run it up over her tighter back entrance. "Tell me, Cookie. Give me a few stats."

She catches her breath as I press into her pretty ass.

"Um..."

"What's that?" I ask, leaning over her, bracing my hand on the mattress, pressing my finger deeper. "I can't hear the impressive list of numbers you're rattling off."

"Two," she pants.

I grin. "Two? Two what?" I slide my finger in and out, then add my thumb against her clit.

She swallows. "Skates. He wears two skates."

I chuckle, press a kiss to her shoulder blade, and move my fingers even deeper. "Yes, he does. You're such a good student, Cookie."

She presses back against my hand. "That feels so good."

"You want more of that?" I move my hand a little faster. I know she does.

"Yes."

"Where do you want me to fill you up, Dani?"

Her head drops forward, and she's breathing faster. She's quickly become a fan of being taken in both places at once. We can't do that tonight, but I will do whatever else she wants me to, and we'll give her as much pleasure as we possibly can.

"God...Michael..."

"Take her ass, Hughes." Nathan shifts, reaching underneath and running his hands along her belly to her clit. "I'll fill up this greedy pussy."

I lean back, and he thrusts three fingers into her at once. She cries out in pleasure, and I wrap a hand around my cock, squeezing.

I run my other hand up her back. "Dani–"

"I'm ready, Michael. *Please*."

Her begging is my weakness.

"Fuck," I mutter. I ease another finger into her, stretching her and making sure she's ready.

"Yes, yes, yes," she's babbling.

Nathan is finger-fucking her hard, and Crew has reached out to play with her nipples.

I spit on my hand, coat my cock, and then line up. I press forward slowly but steadily, filling her.

She presses back against me, taking me. "Michael! Yes!"

My name on her lips makes me have to pause so I don't slam into her. "Fuck, fuck, fuck," I mutter.

She reaches back, grabbing my wrist. "*Please*, Michael."

How the hell am I supposed to do anything else?

"How many hat tricks does Crew have this season, Danielle?" Nate asks.

I see him glance at our hockey star.

Crew lifts his middle finger. Nathan grins.

Danielle, on the other hand, just shakes her head quickly. She already answered this one, but she still says, "No. I don't know. I can't…"

Crew leans in. He wraps her hair around his hand and tips her head back. "Seventeen, pretty girl. That's your number right now."

She tries to shake her head, but I pull out a little and then push back in, and she can't think. I fucking love that.

"That's how many inches of cock you've taken so far, and that makes you a very good girl." He kisses her forehead. "Just let us in."

She whimpers softly, and I pull back and thrust again. Nathan keeps his hand moving. Crew keeps her head up.

Within minutes, my balls are tightening, and I'm going to come.

"Cookie–"

And she comes apart just then, crying out my name, and then Nathan's, then Crew's. I pump my hips and fill her up, my release so fucking satisfying.

I keep hold of her hips as I ease out of her to keep her from falling forward. Crew kisses her again and lets go of her hair. Nathan reaches up and grasps her chin. "Ride me, Danielle."

He's not going to give her even a minute.

He pulls her forward. She straddles his hips. At some point, as

I was losing my mind in her, he freed his cock from his pants, and she immediately starts to sink down on him.

"Oh, God," she murmurs. "I don't know if I can…"

Nathan is gripping her hips, and he presses her down fully. "Take my cock like a good girl, Danielle."

She has a safe word, and it's not *I don't know if I can*.

"Yes, oh, Nathan." She grips his shoulders.

"That's my girl." He's moving her. She's not doing much, but he doesn't seem to mind.

"I don't know anything about hockey right now," she says softly, almost to herself.

"Goddamned right, you don't," Nathan says, picking up their pace.

"Do you even know what day it is?" Crew teases.

"No," she says. "I don't care. I just want…this. All of this, every day."

Mission accomplished in getting our girl out of her head and away from her worries.

Nathan is now thrusting up into her with a furious pace, and soon he's shouting out his release.

Finally, Dani slumps against him, completely spent.

Nathan tucks her face into his shoulder, running his hand up and down her back and resting his head back against the wall. Crew and I both lean back against the walls behind us.

A few minutes pass with all of us just breathing and recovering and appreciating all of *this*.

But eventually Crew looks around and says, "Yes, I know this RV was a brilliant idea. You are all fucking welcome. And yes, I'm happy to be in charge of transportation for all future road trips, holidays, and vacations."

"*No*," Nathan and I say at the same time.

But we're all grinning.

Well, all except Dani.

She's fallen asleep against Nathan.

CHAPTER 11
Michael

I WAKE up on Christmas morning at six, stiff from our cramped sleeping conditions but sighing contentedly. Last night was incredible. I can never get enough of Dani.

Sliding off the couch I moved to after the others fell asleep, I pull on joggers and a sweatshirt. The bedroom is quiet, so I assume everyone else is sleeping, which gives me an opportunity to spend a few minutes with Kevin and Mary by myself.

After stepping into my sneakers, I glance into the bedroom. Dani is in the middle of the bed, her hair a riot of auburn curls in the morning sun peeking through the RV window. She looks beautiful and peaceful, a single slender foot poking out from under the sheet. Crew's hand is resting on her stomach, which has caused the top of the sheet to drag down, exposing the swell of her breast. She's facing Nathan, who is jammed against the wall. Her hand is splayed over his head, as if she was running her fingers through his hair when she dropped off to sleep.

Being with her here is the only Christmas gift I need, but I also can't wait for her to meet my family. I don't expect they'll ask a lot of questions because they assume everyone's relationship is their own business. I just want them to understand and appreciate why I'm in love with Dani and what these two other men offer her.

Which they will, I'm confident of that.

Dani's parents, on the other hand, still need some time and some coaxing.

I figure it won't hurt to butter them up with some pancakes.

Mary comes into the kitchen ten minutes later in a robe and slippers, eyeing me curiously. "Do I smell coffee?"

"You do. Would you like a cup?" I reach for a mug. I've already started the pancake batter I'm making from scratch, and the coffee has just finished brewing.

"I would love one."

"Cream and sugar?"

"Yes, please. Forty years in this house, and I've never once woken up to coffee made for me."

I finish stirring in the sugar and hand her the mug. "Then Merry Christmas, Mary."

She gives a small smile. "Thank you, Michael. Merry Christmas."

"Should I get a cup ready for Kevin?"

"Oh, Kevin is not a morning person." She sips and eyes me over the rim. "Besides, I think he drank way more of that bourbon than he's used to. He was snoring like a freight train all night. I hope it didn't wake you up."

"Not at all," I say smoothly, not willing to admit we all high-tailed it to the RV. "I hope you don't mind me poking around your kitchen and starting some pancakes."

"Michael, no one, and I mean no one, has ever just taken it upon themselves to start cooking in my kitchen without me."

I pause, whisk in hand, concerned that I've now totally offended her.

But Mary sighs. "And I absolutely love it. This is amazing. Thank you."

Relieved, I put the whisk in the eggs and make quick business of them. "I enjoy cooking. I think it's something I learned from my mother. Feeding people is an easy way to show them you care about them."

Mary sets her mug down and moves in beside me. She starts to zest the lemon I pulled out. "I've always felt the same way. Though sometimes I do get tired of doing it by myself. Dani never liked being in the kitchen with me."

"Whenever I'm in town, we can plan to cook together," I tell her, wanting to make it clear that I'm in this with Dani for the long haul.

She nods, but then she says, "To be totally honest, I wish it were just you."

I know what she means, but I want her to spell it out clearly. "What do you mean?"

"I wish Dani was just dating you. You're a lovely, intelligent, nurturing man, and you cook. You're exactly who I always envisioned marrying my daughter."

"I'm flattered. It's a huge compliment to get your stamp of approval, and I don't take that lightly." I really don't. I'm honored she thinks so highly of me already. "But—

Mary cuts me off. "I know. But. There's always a but." She sets down the zester and reaches for her coffee. "It's nothing against Nathan and Crew. They're nice men, and I appreciate how hard they're trying. Please don't mention what I just said. I would never want to upset them or hurt their feelings. I should have kept my thoughts to myself."

She probably should have, but I understand where she's coming from. "I won't mention it." I gesture to the refrigerator, which is sporting a Christmas tree magnet Dani made in grade school. It's very heavy on the glitter. "You know how Dani was always making things as a kid?"

"Yes, like I said last night, she loved to craft, to sew, and to write her little stories. Only she'd never let me read them. She was very creative."

"She still is. She still writes stories. Romances, love stories."

"She does?" Mary looks startled but pleased. "I wonder why she didn't tell me?"

"Because they're love stories that you might not understand."

"Oh." She frowns. "I don't like to think she can't share her creativity with me."

"Dani is very romantic, and her writing reflects that. Why wouldn't she be, right? She sees her parents share a loving, long-lasting marriage, and she's always felt incredibly loved and wanted by the both of you. I think that she was always searching for a love that's big enough to fill that need. To be all-consuming and powerful, and permanent. Instead, she's focused on her writing because she hasn't found one man who could give her all of that."

Mary nods and gives me a knowing smile. "So maybe she needed three men? Is that what you're telling me?"

"Maybe she needed three men." I take a swallow of my own coffee. "Just food for thought."

Mary definitely seems to be thinking about my words. We fall into a comfortable silence that is almost immediately interrupted.

"My fucking head is killing me," Kevin says, stumbling into the kitchen. He bends over the sink and drinks straight from the tap, reminding me a lot of Crew. This is the first time I've heard him swear. I think Nathan's bourbon is the gift that keeps on giving.

"Kevin, good Lord!" Mary says. "Get a glass!"

He stands up and wipes his mouth on his pajama sleeve. "My mouth tastes like I gargled with muddy rocks." He meets my gaze. "Good morning. Merry Christmas."

"Merry Christmas. Coffee?"

He nods. "Thank you." He eyes my mixing bowl. "What's this?"

"Pancakes. Plus, I found some bacon in the fridge I was going to fry."

Kevin claps me on the shoulder. "You're a good man. Even if you went to Purdue."

That makes me laugh. Kevin went to Indiana, our biggest rival. "I am a Boilermaker for life."

I hand him a coffee mug. I don't even ask if he wants cream

and sugar. He strikes me as a man who thinks lattes are a waste of good coffee beans.

He takes it and swallows half the mug. Then he nods in approval. "That will put hair on your chest. Perfect brew, Doc. If I can call you Doc."

"Absolutely. That's what friends and family call me."

Dani has just come in the back door, cheeks pink from the cold, wearing her sweats and slippers. Hearing my words, she pulls the door shut behind her, steps right up to me, and kisses me softly on the lips, breaking her father's no-PDA rule.

To my surprise, neither of her parents say a word of protest, and when Crew comes in behind Dani, Mary goes right up to him and gives him a big hug.

"Merry Christmas, Crew," she says.

He looks startled, but he hugs her back. "Merry Christmas, Mrs. Larkin."

"Call me Mary." She pats him on the cheek.

Crew grins like he's won the Stanley Cup.

Nathan enters the kitchen, his hair sticking up straight, rubbing his jaw. He has beard stubble and looks like he doesn't understand why he has to be awake.

But then Mary reaches out to give his hand a squeeze. "Merry Christmas, Nathan. We're glad you're here."

The cobwebs seem to lift, and his back straightens. He smiles at her. "Merry Christmas, Mary."

"Did I tell you all about the time Danielle played an angel in the Christmas play?" She reaches into the refrigerator and pulls out the bacon. "All those red curls under that halo—it was so cute, I almost couldn't stand it."

"Mom, no one cares."

"Not true," Nathan protests.

"I want to see the pictures," Crew says.

"I bet she was the most angelic of all the angels," I agree, dropping some water on the skillet to test the heat.

Mary beams at all of us. "She really was. But…" Mary's smile turns just a bit mischievous, and I see Dani's face in forty years. "Her halo was a little crooked the entire time."

We all laugh together at that as Dani grins and blushes.

CHAPTER 12
Nathan

"NATHAN, WOULD YOU LIKE MORE COFFEE?" one of Michael's many sisters asks me with a smile.

"I would love some, thank you."

She holds her hand out for my mug, and I pass it over, feeling very content this Christmas day. Danielle slept tucked against me all night, exactly the way I like it, and meeting Michael's family is going even smoother than expected.

Being with the Hughes family is a walk in the damn park after being at the Larkins'. Or even with the McNeills, who while wonderful and welcoming, are… exuberant. Like Crew himself. Full of energy, and questions, and high fives. Danielle's parents were exhausting in their strained disapproval, even if in the end I felt like we'd made some serious progress after my talk with Kevin, Crew's determined enthusiasm, and Michael's cooking skills.

Both previous houses had also felt crowded for different reasons. The McNeills have a large house, but it was stuffed to the gills with family and friends, and everyone had talked loudly and over each other. The Larkins' small house had compartmentalized rooms and too much furniture. Between that and their clear discomfort, the house had felt a little suffocating.

Which was why it was so important to escape to the RV and spend time alone, the four of us, fucking out our frustration. It had been a long, taxing day, with the best possible ending—all of us loving on Danielle.

But I could spend every Christmas with the Hughes family and actually enjoy myself. I don't even care if Michael is there or not, just give me a stocking on the mantle and a seat at the table because this is comfortable to me. Of course, that's not actually true. Part of what is making this Christmas stand out isn't just being around a loving family or spending it with Danielle. It's us. Cookie & Co. My friendship with Michael and Crew is just another layer to the foundation of a different future for myself than I ever imagined.

The coffee mug reappears, and I take it with a thanks, raising it to my lips as I observe the gathering.

It's clear where Michael gets his chill demeanor from because his father, Clayton, is exactly the same. Genuine smile, strong handshake, social but not aggressively so, and easy to talk to. His mother Lorraine is warm, intelligent, and can direct her children with a single look.

Michael has five siblings, three brothers-in-law, and six nieces and nephews, yet nothing feels chaotic or crowded in the ranch-style home filled with books and landscape artwork that I've been told was done by Clayton's mother. The Christmas decor is classic red and very elegant, with ceramic angels and a large hand-carved nativity scene. It's the complete opposite of the plastic Christmas emporium Crew turned Dani's apartment into. The poinsettia I brought fits perfectly in the Hughes' home.

The food covers the entire length of the buffet table, and my mouth is already watering just eyeing it all. I barely ate last night or this morning because when I'm tense, I can't swallow, so I'm starving now.

I'm sitting on the sofa between Michael's sister, Tonya, and her son, who is seven, who keeps eyeing me with a half-smile, like something about me is cracking him up.

The other kids are all downstairs in the finished basement, with one of Michael's brothers-in-law supervising. I occasionally hear running, or a thump, or a cheer coming up the stairs, which makes me think there are obstacle courses in play down there.

Danielle is in a wingback chair across from me, holding Michael's other sister, Becca's baby, Braydon Junior. I've been told he's six months old, and he is sporting a toothless grin, round cheeks, and a full head of hair. He's wearing a tiny rowing sweater that matches his father's, along with baby khakis. He's pretty fucking cute.

Watching Danielle smile at him, pure joy on her face, is making my heart squeeze. She looks natural holding a baby.

"Nathan, I've heard you have a stunning view from your apartment," Clayton says, popping a handful of pistachios in his mouth. "Do you like living downtown?"

"I do, actually," I say, wrenching my eyes away from our sweet girl to focus on Michael's father. "It's very convenient for work, and I like the sounds of the city."

"I always wanted to try out city life, but Lorraine's career was really taking off at the university here, so we settled in. It was a good place to have a family, though. I can't imagine raising kids in downtown Chicago."

"I really can't imagine that either, though lots of people do. I grew up in Winnetka, in the suburbs. Well, until I was twelve." When my parents died. That's not a topic for a happy Christmas lunch, though. "I'm impressed that you both managed your careers and raised six kids."

Michael's mother is a Lit professor, and his father is now retired but was a CPA.

"Oh, that's all credit to Lorraine," he says with a smile directed at his wife. "She has endless energy and is the most hardworking woman I know. Smart as a whip. She can manage circles around me."

"Then my question is for you, Lorraine. What's your secret? To having a career and raising a wonderful family?"

She takes the hand her husband offers her and smiles at me. "Patience. Being organized, very organized. Giving love and hugs and making time to eat dinner together. And respect. You have to both give it to your children and demand it in return."

"I think it's obvious you've accomplished that." This *is* a family filled with love and respect. That's very clear.

"Remember when Tonya called you a dictator, Mom?" Becca says, running her hand over her baby's head as she walks past. She gives her sister an amused look.

"Why are you bringing that up?" Tonya asks, though she doesn't sound angry. "I was twelve, and I wanted to stay out later. I think that's totally normal at that age."

"Oh, I remember that," Lorraine says. "You thought you were grown and should be allowed to run around until midnight. I told you this was not a democracy, and you got no vote. You had two choices. You could be home by ten or not go out at all."

"What did you do?" I ask Tonya. Michael told us she's four years younger than him and a statistical analyst, which makes me instantly like her. "Besides call her a dictator."

"I didn't say that in front of her, just to be clear. I don't have a death wish. Her eagle ears overheard me in my room." She shakes her head at me. "Nathan, can you believe that I thought I would "show my mom" and just stay home? Like I was punishing her and not myself. So, then all my friends were out having a good time, and I was watching cartoons with my baby brother. And I had to write an essay on the difference between dictatorship and democracy."

"Hey, I'm good company," the youngest Hughes sibling, Garrett, says. He's a student at Northwestern, though I didn't catch what he's studying.

"I like hanging out with you," George, Tonya's son, pipes up.

"I like hanging out with you too," Garrett says, giving George a fist bump.

George turns and gives me a look of triumph. I smile at him, and he frowns. I've never spent a lot of time around kids. Not even when I was a kid. I have no idea what to say to him. "You like hockey?" I ask him.

He shakes his head. "No."

So that topic is a dead end. I'm kind of amused by his honesty.

"George," his mother reprimands. "Mr. Armstrong owns a hockey team, and Mr. McNeill is a pro hockey player."

"Well, I still don't like hockey."

"George, come help me in the kitchen," Lorraine says, giving him The Look.

George pops off the sofa instantly and follows, though he eyes me like it's my fault he's probably in trouble.

"Do you have kids?" Becca asks me.

"Me?" God, I hate this question. I'm sure I have "childless middle-aged rich man" written all over me, so I'm always surprised people even ask me. "No."

"We always thought Michael would be the first to have kids," Tonya says. "He was like our second father. Very patient, always the mediator when we weren't getting along. When he wasn't reading, that is. He constantly had his nose in a book."

"He's still like that," I say. "He keeps me and Crew from killing each other."

"It's always Nathan's fault," Crew calls out from where he's playing checkers with Braydon Senior in the corner.

Michael, who has been in the kitchen busily prepping something, as if the buffet actually needs any more food, comes into the family room. He's wearing a Christmas apron that says "Cookie Crew," the irony of which is not lost on me. He sets a platter down on the straining sideboard.

"It's both your faults," he says, leaning over to tickle Braydon Junior on the cheek, then kisses Danielle on the top of the head before returning to the kitchen.

Michael told us we could feel comfortable around his family touching Danielle, as long as it is respectful affection, and not overtly sexual. A hand on the small of the back is cool, but no ass pats. I think that's fair for a family gathering. No one has asked us much about our relationship. They seem to accept it for what it is, and I appreciate that tremendously.

Danielle stands up with the baby and smooths down the green dress she's wearing. She comes over and faces Braydon out, bouncing him in front of me. "Do you want to hold the baby?"

"Uh…"

No. The answer is no. I've only held a baby maybe twice in my life, and both times they cried. But it seems rude to refuse. "I guess, but only if he wants me to."

Danielle laughs. "Just put your arms around him when I set him on your lap."

I'm mildly panicking. My back stiffens, and I hold my breath when she puts the baby down, facing me. I put one arm around his back and put my opposite hand squarely on his waist, terrified he'll topple onto the floor. In spite of my nerves, Braydon smiles at me, drool slipping down his chin.

Damn. This kid instantly owns me.

"He's very cute," I say to Becca.

"Thank you," Braydon Senior calls out. "I did that."

Becca snorts.

Braydon Junior and I check each other out. He stares at me with big brown eyes, and something shifts and cracks inside me. He's freaking adorable. I relax a little and start to make faces at him. "Hey, little man. Do you like hockey?"

He grins at me and gives me a sweet little coo.

"Definitely likes hockey," I report, glancing up at Danielle.

The look on her face makes me fall in love with her all over again. She's beaming watching the baby. There is so much love in her that she's glowing with it. I didn't think she could be any more beautiful than she already is, but seeing her joy at being here, on Christmas, with us and Michael's welcoming family, watching me hold a little chubby baby, I don't think I've ever seen her look more radiant.

Our eyes lock, and I try to convey everything that I feel for her, for us, for this moment. Her eyes widen, and her bottom lip drops so her mouth forms a perfect "o."

"Wow," Tonya says, which snaps me out of it.

I glance over at her, then quickly back at the baby when I see Tonya's amusement. My heart is racing. Braydon raises his arms up and down.

"I think Dani's plan worked perfectly," Tonya said.

I frown. "What plan?"

She chuckles. "A woman doesn't hand her man a baby unless she has plans."

Instantly, I'm lifting the baby and shoving him back into Danielle's arms. I jump off the sofa and narrowly miss kicking over the coffee mug I set on the floor.

"Nathan," Danielle says, concern in her voice.

"Did I say something wrong?" Tonya asks. "I'm sorry. I didn't mean to make you uncomfortable."

"It's fine," I tell Tonya. "I just need a coffee warmer." I grab the mug off the floor.

I give Danielle a tight smile to let her know it's okay and make my way into the kitchen. Instinctively, I seek out Michael as I set my mug down on the counter. He's become my emotional touchstone. True to form, he reaches out and claps me on the shoulder.

"Here." He puts an oven mitt in my hand. "Pull the au gratin potatoes out of the oven for me."

While I yank open the oven door, he moves in next to me under the guise of stirring a pot on the stove. "I'm sorry about that. You okay?"

I nod. "I'm fine." I lift the heavy casserole dish and set it on the stove.

"We should talk about this later," he murmurs.

I nod again. "Sure."

I want to say there's nothing to talk about. I can't give Danielle a baby, now or at any point in the future. But this isn't just about me. This is about all of us. Where we're going and what we're doing.

Christmas has really brought it home that we need to discuss what we all want. Now and later.

I've never wanted kids. I don't even know why I'm upset.

Maybe because the idea that I can't give Danielle something she might want makes me feel like shit. But I remind myself that even if I can't meet all of Danielle's needs, there are two other men in this relationship. That's something pretty damn special.

"I'm really happy to be here," I tell Michael truthfully. "Your family is awesome."

"They are. But, fair warning, I think my mother has decided to adopt you. I've never seen her pat a newcomer's arm as much as she has yours."

That makes me feel ridiculously pleased. I want Michael's parents to like me. "It was the poinsettia. It won her over."

Michael chuckles. "It didn't hurt. Do you think we have enough food?" he asks with a grin.

"I'm going to destroy everything in sight. It all looks amazing. Then I'm going to need to hit the gym first thing tomorrow. Care to join me?"

"I would love to." Michael pats his gut. "I lied. I've been eating cookies all week."

"You weren't fooling anyone," I tell him. "Crew isn't the only one with a sweet tooth, and we all know it."

Lorraine comes up behind us. She rubs my back with the palm of her hand, and it makes me feel pretty damn good.

Michael gives me a "I told you" look.

"Do you two have everything ready in here?" Lorraine asks.

"Michael? Anything else we need to do?"

"No, I think we're ready to eat."

"Isn't he fantastic in the kitchen?" his mother asks, clearly proud of her son.

"Mom," Michael says, chuckling softly. "What's he supposed to say to that?"

"What? I'm allowed to brag on my son. The *doctor*. Who also cooks."

"He definitely keeps us in pancakes," I tell Lorraine. "And he's slowly breaking Crew of his dependence on Pop Tarts."

"Then I have even more reason to be proud of him." Lorraine takes a bowl of biscuits and departs. She calls down the basement steps, "Time to eat!"

My phone buzzes in my pocket. I wouldn't even look at it, except I see Michael's phone light up on the counter at the same time. It's from Danielle.

"What does that say?" he asks.

I hold his phone up so we can both read it.

> No one panic. I do NOT want a baby right now.

Crew responds.

> #17 to Cookie&Co: Thank God. lol.

Michael quickly types.

> Doc to Cookie&Co: No one is panicking. Just enjoy Christmas.

> Boss to Cookie&Co: I never panic.

Then I realize I have another text I didn't notice earlier. I read it and actually laugh out loud.

It's from Wade, our Racketeers mascot. Who has clearly been hitting the eggnog. Or more likely, he's been popping edibles.

> Merry Christmas, ya filthy animal! This is your OFFICIAL Sammy, the malamute. Thanks for the bonus! I hope you're getting your balls jingled and you're feeling that big Nick energy with your girl. Say hi to Dr. Hughes and McNeill for me.

Then there's a nutcracker emoji and #crushinit.

The only thing Wade is officially is an idiot.

I forward it to our Cookie & Co. group text. I have a feeling Wade is going to regret sending that, so I text him back, so he doesn't wake up tomorrow terrified I'll fire him.

> Merry Christmas to you too. See you at the game Thursday, and never mention my balls ever again.

Crew comes jogging into the kitchen. "Boss is laughing? It's a Christmas miracle."

I roll my eyes, but I don't mean it. I catch Danielle's eye and give her a big smile, then kiss her on the cheek.

One more text, and then my phone is going back in my pocket for the rest of the day.

> Boss to Cookie & Co: I'm glad I'm spending the holidays with my favorite people. I love you all. Even Crew.

Then I shove my phone away and whistle Jingle Bells as I carry the potatoes to the table.

Kids come racing up the steps and tumble into the family room, and someone yells at them to wash their hands. Adults are talking and laughing, and music is playing.

It's the best Christmas I've had in a very long time.

CHAPTER 13
Crew

DAMN, I really love Nathan's shower.

I did not spill my extra large soda on myself in the RV on purpose. But the fact that I need to jump in the shower when we all get back to Nathan's apartment doesn't make me mad.

I slip into his bathrobe too. Because why not? Yeah, my bag is right outside the door, but I've worn most of what's in it and… Nathan has great taste in just about everything. Coffee, sports drinks, women, bathrobes.

I'm tightening the belt as I step out into the living room. I just stop in the doorway for a moment. My little family is here, and they've all crashed hard.

Michael is puttering around in the kitchen, storing leftovers.

Nathan is stretched out on the couch, with Dani on top of him. His eyes are closed, his tie and shoes are off, and though his hand is resting on her back, it's not moving.

I come around the end of the couch and glance down at my girl. Her eyes are open, but she's staring dreamily at the white Christmas lights on the fireplace mantle.

I run my hand over her hair. She gives me a sweet smile.

I drop onto the end of the other couch.

She moves her head so she can look at me. "You're wearing his robe?"

"You can't scold me for this since you didn't join me in the shower."

She smiles, then yawns. "I wouldn't have done a good job soaping you up. I'm exhausted."

"There's no such thing as a bad job soaping me up," I say with a chuckle. But honestly, I'm not sure I have the energy to put her up against the shower wall. It's probably for the best that she crashed out here. I motion with my hand. "Come here."

She carefully removes Nathan's hand from her back and slips off of him. He grunts softly but doesn't open his eyes. She comes over to me and climbs up into my lap, tucking her knees underneath her skirt. She cuddles into my chest, resting her head on my shoulder.

I wrap my arms around her and just breathe in her scent.

"I should probably go home soon," I tell her. "Game tomorrow."

She sighs. "I understand. I wish you didn't have to leave."

I do too. We all spend a lot of time together, and it's not that I'm not comfortable here. But all my gear is at my place, and to really be in the right headspace before a game, I'm best when I can crank my music and zone out a little. No matter how much time we all spend here, this is still Nathan's place.

"You can come home with me," I say to Dani. I definitely sleep better when she's with me.

The other guys say the same.

She nods. "Maybe I will."

"No," Nathan says from the couch.

Of course, he wasn't totally asleep.

"Why do you get to keep her?" I ask.

For the most part, when Dani and I sleep together…and when we *sleep together*… it's here at Nathan's. But just like I've taken her to the movies by myself and Michael's taken her to museums, just the two of them, she has spent the night with both of us alone at our places a couple of times.

But I won't lie, it feels weird. We have a great time. If it were just me and Dani together forever, I'd be perfectly happy. But if I'm totally honest, there's something missing when the other two aren't there.

"Because I call dibs," Nathan says.

Dani giggles, and I grin. "I said it first, so *I* get dibs," I tell him.

"Nope. Mine."

"What do you think dibs is?" I ask.

"I think dibs is when the guy who signs the paychecks wants something and gets it."

I laugh and stroke my hand up and down Dani's thigh. I just want to touch her. I'm not even up for sex, which is something I never say. But these four Christmases were a lot. And, though I will never admit this out loud, sleeping in that RV last night kind of sucked.

"I wish you could just stay so I can have you all here," Dani says softly.

"He can stay," Nathan says. "Hell, he's already in my bathrobe."

"Does this mean I get to keep it?" I ask him. "My naked balls are all over it, just so you know."

Nathan looks at Dani. "If I had a problem touching things that your naked balls touch, we'd all be in a very different situation." Then he winks at her.

She and I both laugh.

Damn, exhausted Nathan is funny.

"I'm still keeping it," I say, pulling one side of the robe more tightly around me. "I'll consider it my Christmas gift."

Michael comes into the room and hands me a plate with a sandwich. Turkey, but he did something fancy by including dressing and cranberry sauce on the sandwich. And I think I see gravy too.

"Thanks, Doc."

"You know, our idea not to exchange gifts was a good one," Michael comments as he sinks down onto the couch next to Dani and me and reaches for one of her feet, pulling it over into his lap. He lifts half a sandwich and bites into it.

Nathan nods. "You are all impossible to buy for."

Dani laughs. "That's probably because you all are millionaires, and you buy me stuff all the time for no reason."

I kiss her head. "The reason is we love you and want to spoil you, and don't think that's going to stop anytime soon."

"And I'm actually a billionaire," Nathan says.

Just then, Nathan's phone dings with a text, and he reaches into his pocket to pull it out. He reads something on the screen. Then smiles. "We now have a house to stay in when we go to Franklin."

Michael shakes his head. "I thought we agreed you wouldn't call your real estate agent on Christmas."

"I didn't call him. I texted him. And I waited until this evening. Christmas is practically over."

Dani sits up a little straighter and looks at him. "You bought a house in Franklin? By text?"

"My agent knows what I like. And there aren't that many houses in Franklin that meet my standards," he says as he closes his eyes again.

Michael chuckles. "How many were there that were good enough for Nathan Armstrong?"

Nathan's eyes are still closed, but he smiles. "One."

We all laugh.

"Does it have a barn?" Michael asks.

"It does, as a matter of fact," Nathan says. "Hey, Crew, do you want a pony?"

"Hell yeah," I say. "Who doesn't want a pony?"

"Grown-assed men," Nathan says.

"You don't need a barn, and Crew doesn't need a pony," Michael says.

I shrug. "It's not about need, Doc. You heard Nate. It's about *want*. Maybe I want a pony." I really don't. But I enjoy messing with Nathan.

"Well, you'll have to buy your own pony. But you can keep it in my barn."

"You're such a dirty-talker, Boss," I tell him, taking a big bite of my sandwich.

Nathan just shakes his head. He doesn't even bother flipping me off or anything. He really is tired.

"You know," Michael says in that thoughtful, I-have-a-fantastic-idea voice of his. "While you're in the real estate buying mood, we should talk about something."

Nathan opens his eyes at that and tucks a hand behind his head. "Something like what?"

Oh, sure, he'll pay full attention when *Doc* talks.

I just grin and keep eating.

Michael is rubbing his hand up and down Dani's calf, and he looks over at us. "I think we'd all agree that we would prefer to all be here together all the time."

Nathan snorts.

"Okay, eighty-seven percent of the time," Michael corrects.

I shoot Nathan a look. He doesn't argue with that, and I smile.

"What are you saying?" Dani asks. Her eyes are wide.

"I think we proved with all these Christmases, meeting each other's families, and showing that we are a united front no matter what, that we're serious. About each other. About this relationship. About doing this long-term," Michael says.

"I definitely am," I say.

"Yes," Nathan says simply.

Dani's blinking rapidly now, but she nods.

"So, it just makes sense that we start looking for a place where all four of us can live. Together. Full-time."

Whoa. That's…fast.

But I want it. I know that immediately. My chest feels warm, and I hug Dani tighter.

Never kissing Dani goodbye at Nathan's door? Never going

back to my empty, lonely apartment by myself? Knowing when I come home from being on the road, Dani will always be there?

"I'm in," I say.

We all look over at Nathan.

He's got his phone up in front of his face.

"Nathan?" Dani asks quietly.

He looks over. "My agent says that he can send some listings over to us in a couple of days. We just need to let him know what specifications we have."

We all look at one another. Michael grins. I say, "fuck yeah," and then add, "hot tub." And Nathan just puts his phone back in his pocket.

And then Dani bursts into tears.

We all react like we always do to her tears. We all lean in with frowns.

"Cookie?" Michael asks.

I squeeze her tighter. "What's wrong?"

"Danielle," Nathan's voice is firm, but he's sitting up now.

But she's shaking her head. "Nothing's wrong. I'm so happy." She gives us each a bright smile. "*This* is what I wanted for Christmas."

We all look at her.

Nathan pulls in a breath. "Jesus, why didn't you just tell us that?"

"Because you all had to get to this point by yourselves," she says, dashing the tears off her cheeks. "I know that you would've said yes. You all always do everything to make me happy. But you all had to decide this is what you wanted too."

"It is what we want," Michael says, leaning over and kissing her knee.

"Definitely. Definitely want it," I say against her temple.

"Me too," Nathan says, his voice a little gruff. He clears his throat. "But we're getting a place with four rooms. Even if we don't sleep separately, everybody needs their own space." He looks right at me. "We're not sharing a closet."

I grin at him. "As long as we can share a shower."

Nathan groans. "When you say it like that, it sounds like we're *in* the shower together."

I just wiggle my brows at him.

Nathan narrows his eyes. "You know that's never going to happen right?"

I realize that I am a lot more laid back about sex and sexuality than Nathan will ever be. And I need to respect that. I nod. "Yes, Boss, I know."

"I just want to be sure no one gets confused," Nathan says.

I make sure he sees that I'm sincere when I say, "I know. I get it. I promise I won't tease anymore."

Nathan nods, and I can already read him well enough to know that he believes me.

"Here at home, it's funny. As long as you don't say stuff like that in front of anybody else at the Racketeers. Or on social media. Or our families. Or in public at all."

I grin. "Got it. You keep me in bougie shampoo and body wash, and I'll keep my mouth shut about where I use it."

Nathan shakes his head as if he's maybe already regretting this new living arrangement idea. "You're a fucking millionaire. You could buy your own shampoo and body wash," he tells me. As he always does.

I hug Dani closer and kiss her head again. "Yeah, but it's so fun having a sugar daddy, isn't it Dani?"

Michael laughs. "Watch yourself, McNeill." He lifts his sandwich for another bite. "At least until we have the papers signed on our new place. Then he won't be able to get rid of you."

Not that Nathan would kick me out—he'd miss me whether he'll admit it or not. But damn, *our* new place sounds really fucking good.

"I can't believe this is happening," Dani says. "I love you all so much."

"What do you want in a new apartment?" I ask Dani, sweeping my fingers over her red curls.

"I don't know. I haven't thought about it."

"You need a writing room," Michael says. "Like an office and reading room combination."

"Dani needs her own bathroom," Nathan points out.

"I think she needs a pony."

But Dani snuggles in closer against my chest. "All I need is the three of you. Merry Christmas to me."

I feel a wave of contentment wash over me.

My eyes land on the Christmas stockings with our initials that Dani hung on Nathan's sleek and modern fireplace. New traditions for Cookie & Co.

I can't wait for the next step.

About the Author

Emma Foxx is the super fun and sexy pen name for two long-time, bestselling romance authors who decided why have just one hero when you can have three at the same time? (they're not sure what took them so long to figure this out)! Emma writes contemporary romances that will make you laugh (yes, maybe out loud in public) and want more…books (sure, that's what we mean 😉). Find Emma on Instagram, Tik Tok, and Goodreads.

Also by Emma Foxx

Puck One Night Stands (Book One Chicago Racketeers)

Seriously Pucked (Book Three Chicago Racketeers)

Dani and her guys take the next step in their relationship… moving in together.

And read the final book in Dani, Crew, Michael, and Nathan's love story, Permanently Pucked (Book Four Chicago Racketeers!)

Milton Keynes UK
Ingram Content Group UK Ltd.
UKHW040845131024
449481UK00004B/198